Thérèse Desqueyroux

Thérèse Desqueyroux

FRANÇOIS MAURIAC

TRANSLATION, INTRODUCTION, AND NOTES BY
RAYMOND N. MACKENZIE

FOREWORD BY JOSEPH CUNNEEN

A SHEED & WARD BOOK

ROWMAN & LITTLEFIELD PUBLISHERS, INC.
Lanham • Boulder • New York • Toronto • Oxford

A SHEED & WARD BOOK

ROWMAN & LITTLEFIELD PUBLISHERS, INC.

Published in the United States of America
by Rowman & Littlefield Publishers, Inc.
A wholly owned subsidiary of The Rowman & Littlefield Publishing Group, Inc.
4501 Forbes Boulevard, Suite 200, Lanham, Maryland 20706
www.rowmanlittlefield.com

PO Box 317
Oxford
OX2 9RU, UK

British Library Cataloguing in Publication Information Available

Library of Congress Cataloging-in-Publication Data

Mauriac, François, 1885–1970.
  [Thérèse Desqueyroux. English]
  Thérèse Desqueyroux / François Mauriac ; translated by Raymond N. MacKenzie.
      p. cm.
  "A Sheed & Ward book".
  Includes bibliographical references.
  ISBN 0-7425-4864-3 (cloth : alk. paper) — ISBN 0-7425-4865-1 (pbk. : alk. paper)
  I. MacKenzie, Raymond N. II. Title.

PQ2625.A93T513 2005
843'.912—dc22   2004028427

Printed in the United States of America

Contents

Foreword

W hat a splendid idea to go back to Mauriac! Two generations have grown up since he won the Nobel Prize for Literature, and few in America today realize how widely he was read, and how greatly he was revered—and reviled—at the time he was elected to the Académie française in 1934. One can only hope that Raymond MacKenzie's fine new translation of *Thérèse Desqueyroux*, along with his authoritative introduction to the novel, will bring a host of new readers to Mauriac, as well as remind those who have already encountered his work to check their local libraries to look up translations of many of his other books.

Because Mauriac brought honest expression to the repressed passions of his central characters, giving voice to what he later discussed as the "anguish of the Christian life," many French Catholic readers in the 1920s considered his work disloyal and dangerous. Although a committed Catholic from his childhood in Bordeaux—his thesis for his *license ès lettres* was "The Origins of Franciscanism in France"—he had no intention of contributing to the pious literature approved by the *bien-pensants* of his day. The heroes of most of his early novels are writers still in the process of discovering their vocation. Mauriac's acknowledgment that Thérèse, an unhappy woman who tried to poison her husband, is in many ways himself indicates the deep tensions present in his best work.

"I am not a Catholic novelist," he declared at the height of the controversy surrounding his fiction, "I am a Catholic who writes novels." Mauriac's fiction returns again and again to Bordeaux and his youth. "I rediscover," he stated, "the narrow Jansenist world of my devout, unhappy and introverted childhood." Later he was to embrace a more tolerant Christianity, less obsessed with a negative view of sexuality and more concerned with fostering a just and humanist society, but in Thérèse his heroine remains a tortured figure.

This edition of the novel is especially helpful in adding Mauriac's first narrative effort to present his heroine, "Conscience, the Divine Instinct." This takes the form of an imaginary letter from Thérèse to her confessor; the novelist's earliest intention was to present her as a believer who is consciously working out her salvation. In the finished novel, however, she shares her father's rejection of Christianity, and has no sympathy for the "correct" practice of her husband and his family. When she is forced to attend Sunday Mass with them, however, she is somewhat drawn to the voice and mannerisms of the parish priest, identifying especially with his loneliness. The translator, I believe, has made a wise decision for this book, omitting three later short pieces in which Mauriac returned to Thérèse. In the last of these, "End of the Night," the unhappy woman finally submits to God, an ending which was sharply criticized by Jean-Paul Sartre as artificially imposed, a bad example of authorial omniscience.

In any case, Thérèse's story is a striking instance of Mauriac's criticism of the hypocrisy of bourgeois Catholicism in early twentieth-century France. The Bordeaux world he is describing is not far removed from that narrow nationalism and callous anti-Semitism exhibited a generation earlier during the Dreyfus affair. Respectability substituted for Christianity, and the desire to combine large landholdings made two families rush to insure Thérèse's marriage to Bernard Desqueyroux. What gives Mauriac's presentation of his heroine added depth is her realization that she too is attracted by the idea of owning hundreds of additional acres of pine forests. Though she is extremely intelligent, a constant reader, perhaps a frustrated writer, she does not question the economic order of her society, and enters into marriage as an inevitable fate. Clearly, opportunities for educated women have greatly increased since the 1920s, but an alert reader should be able to see that Mauriac's criticisms apply even today to all those who would reduce the demands of the spirit to conformity with the social imperatives of the world around them.

Though Mauriac is no feminist, he identifies deeply with Thérèse, a woman manipulated by her society, in which the family controls her whole life, and where she can find no one to whom she is able to unburden herself. Her mother died when she was an infant; her father ignores her, totally absorbed by his hope to rise in local politics; her aunt Clara, a surrogate mother figure, is devoted to her but almost totally deaf. The world around Thérèse is completely stifling, but her emotions remain deeply affected by the scent of pine trees and the sundrenched landscape of the Landes.

Although the author shows his debt to Dostoyevsky and Freud, he remains a disciple of Racine in his classical restraint and concentration of dramatic action. He even suggests a connection between Thérèse and Racine's Phaedra, including an ambiguous reflection by the heroine about her "rustic Hippolytus." What is especially striking, as she travels home after her trial preparing for an encounter with her husband, is both the intelligence at work in analyzing her situation and her inability to come to any clear conclusions. Why had she married Bernard? What could enable her to breathe more easily?

There are no pat answers. Thérèse has committed a crime and undergoes an excruciating process of self-understanding. She must work out her existence in a world in which women can only be mothers, wives, old maids, or prostitutes. Marrying her husband had seemed natural in great part because his younger sister, Anne, was the closest companion of her childhood. As a young girl Anne possessed the charm of innocence, but she was extremely naïve, and easily taken in by the superficial charm of Jean Azevedo. The latter, though shallow, had a certain appeal for Thérèse by confirming her independence and suggesting the possibility of a different life in Paris.

Thérèse is narcissistic, shocking the family by apparent disinterest even in her own child, Marie. If she is also a criminal, it is worth keeping in mind that Mauriac calls the very writing of a book a violent act. It is also important that, despite Thérèse's passionate nature, her revolt against her husband was not because she desired another man; her act was an instinctive and desperate attempt to break out of the limitations of her existence. The novel, beginning near the end of her story, observes her deep suffering, through which she perhaps arrives at a new level of self-understanding. Wisely, Mauriac does not try to answer the deep questions his novel raises. It is up to readers to resolve the mystery of its ending, with Thérèse on the sidewalk of a Parisian street, about to begin a new life.

Joseph Cunneen

Introduction

François Mauriac (1885–1970) published twenty-four novels in the course of his life, along with four plays, four volumes of poetry, numerous volumes of biography, and many volumes of criticism and journalism. Yet out of this huge body of work, the one title that remains his best-known work, both in France and outside it, is *Thérèse Desqueyroux*. One reason for this may be its sheer accessibility and emotional impact: few readers will fail to be moved by Thérèse and her plight. And many of us will recognize certain aspects of her character in ourselves—as Mauriac himself did. Thérèse can be seen as an existential heroine, before that term became fashionable, desperately trying to make sense of herself and her actions in a world profoundly alien to her. But direct as the novel's appeal to us is, it is also a book that richly repays careful, repeated readings. It is the most poetic of Mauriac's works, in the sense that it communicates more by imagery and implication than by statement. It is a novel of beautifully layered language, with not a wasted word, but it is also a novel of gaps, silences, and mysteries.

Mauriac first published *Thérèse Desqueyroux* serially in the magazine *Revue de Paris* (from November 15, 1926, to January 1, 1927), and in book form in 1927. At this point in his career, Mauriac's reputation was higher than it had ever been. He had left his native Bordeaux in 1906 to make his way as a writer in Paris. His first book was a volume of conventional and pious poetry titled *Les Mains jointes* (Joined Hands). Published at his own expense, the book would have been a highly inauspicious beginning, but it caught the attention of Maurice Barrès, a highly influential writer and politician. Barrès gave the book a very warm review in the newspaper *Echo de Paris* in March 1910, and Mauriac's career was launched. What followed, however, was a series of respectable but rather derivative novels published between 1913 and 1921, resulting in unspectacular reviews and sales.

All that changed in 1922, with the publication of *Le Baiser au lépreux* (A Kiss for the Leper)—his first book, Mauriac later recalled, to sell more than three thousand copies.[1] With this novel, Mauriac entered upon the psychological and spiritual landscape that would dominate all his later work; he had at last found his own voice and his own subject: the psychological and spiritual analysis of tormented, often despairing souls, their stories played out in the arid Landes region of France. The novels that followed—especially *Génitrix* in 1923 and *Le Désert de l'amour* (The Desert of Love) in 1925—won him an ever-widening audience, an audience whose taste, both in France and throughout Europe and America, was strongly in favor of the sort of writers Gertrude Stein had famously dubbed the "lost generation." The literary masterworks of the 1920s across Europe and America were, with some few major exceptions, expressions of spiritual defeat, of a civilization that had failed. In the English-speaking world, T. S. Eliot's *The Waste Land* (1922) was the defining document. Mauriac's novels of the 1920s, with their alienated and desperate characters moving through a desert-like modern world, felt of a piece with this new pessimistic mood. Mauriac's novels would have felt, in short, like products of the literary movement we now call modernism. Nicholas Hewitt describes the three chief themes of 1920s French modernism as the crisis of civilization (brought on by World War I), the crisis in ethical values, and a sense of the absence of God.[2] To differing degrees, Mauriac's works of the decade all involve these themes and were received as such by contemporary readers.

But while he was being applauded as one of the new masters of the novel, Mauriac was also experiencing an increasing conflict. He was being attacked in the Catholic press as a writer obsessed with unhealthy and degraded characters and perverse psychology. What the secular reader could applaud as Mauriac's unflinching and bold examination of the modern psyche, the Catholic could condemn as a sort of wallowing in sinfulness. Charles Du Bos, a contemporary Catholic critic highly sympathetic to Mauriac, said that between 1922 and 1928, Mauriac the novelist galloped ahead in achievement—but not Mauriac the Catholic.[3] This conflict between the artist and the man of faith was still developing when Mauriac came to write *Thérèse Desqueyroux*, and it would lead to a period of personal crisis during the next several years following the novel.[4]

As we will see below, certain aspects of *Thérèse Desqueyroux* suggest that Mauriac was struggling with his faith—or at least the way some of his critics were expressing that faith; in some respects, Mauriac seems to be using this novel to respond to his Catholic critics by defying them. But to regard *Thérèse Desqueyroux* as either non- or anti-Catholic is to misread it; a more careful reading will reveal it as, on the contrary, a novel saturated in a deep, searching Catholicism, with a challenging and ultimately triumphant vision of a world penetrated to the core with God and grace.

The story of Thérèse has deep roots in Mauriac's life. In Bordeaux in 1905–1906, the newspapers were dominated by the scandal involving Madame Henriette-Blanche Canaby. She was accused of having attempted to poison her husband and of having forged prescriptions for toxic substances—aconite, digitalis, and chloroform. Her husband had been taking a legitimate prescription treatment, Fowler's drops—a medication that included small amounts of arsenic. He became sick, then worsened, and eventually the doctors determined he was suffering from arsenic poisoning. But he refused to testify against his wife, and none of the other poisons were found in his system. All these details, of course, were imported by Mauriac for the story of Bernard's poisoning. Madame Canaby was acquitted of the charge of attempted murder, but she was sentenced to fifteen months in prison for her forgeries.[5] When Mauriac came to write his novel some twenty years later, many of the details—except the conviction—found their way into his story. He pointed out the connection between *Thérèse Desqueyroux* and the Canaby trial himself:

> Among many sources for *Thérèse Desqueyroux* there was certainly the vision I had, at eighteen years of age, in a courtroom,

of a thin woman poisoner between two policemen. I remembered the testimony of the witnesses, and I made use of the story about the forged prescriptions the accused had made use of to obtain her poisons. But that was the point where my borrowings from reality stopped. Taking what reality could furnish me, I was going to create a totally different, more complicated character. The accused's motives had been, in fact, of the most banal kind—she loved a man other than her husband. This was not at all the case with my Thérèse, whose drama consists in herself not knowing what moved her to the criminal act.[6]

The novel does not, however, simply take the real-life Madame Canaby and complicate her: certain essential traits of Thérèse amount to a kind of self-portrait. The novel's preface insists on how well the author knows her, and the epigraph from Baudelaire also calls for sympathy with the "creature" we are about to meet. Mauriac often referred to his own connection with Thérèse, notably in an article written in 1935. There, he says:

We are of the same spiritual race ... and from childhood we were accustomed to examine our hearts, to bring light to bear on our thoughts, our desires, our acts, our omissions. We know that evil is an immense fund of capital shared out among all people, and that there is nothing in the criminal heart, no matter how horrible, whose germ is not also to be found in our own hearts.[7]

This connection between himself and his character was not at first clear to Mauriac, and the novel grew into its present shape over several drafts. The first draft, "Conscience, instinct divin," is presented here as an appendix, and a comparison of the draft with the finished novel is highly instructive. In "Conscience," Mauriac was working with a much simpler, flatter conception of Thérèse—though she is already highly articulate and introspective. This early Thérèse is not an atheist but a practicing Catholic, and she is concerned entirely with repentance for her feelings, especially for her lack of love for her husband. There is greater emphasis on her love for Raymonde—the girl who would become Anne de la Trave in the final novel. A repressed lesbianism dominates this first version of Thérèse's character, and this survives into the novel's final form, though it is no longer the single key to her character, and perhaps not even among the more important ones. But perhaps the most important difference between "Conscience" and the final novel resides in the freedom Mauriac allowed his character to develop, to become herself, and to go her own way. Eva Kushner puts the difference very clearly, saying that in "Conscience," Mauriac can be accused

> [of] leading his heroine to repentance in a quasi-automatic way, taking no account of the complexity of conscience. True, in the brief space of [the draft] the writer has scarcely enough time to make this complexity felt; but he can, nevertheless, suggest it. Now, it is precisely this total lack of nuance that characterizes the fragment "Conscience." Here, Thérèse is a spiritually docile Christian confessing, in writing, to a priest, with no murderous intentions toward her husband, only reproaching him for being unable to make her love him. More than her intellectual superiority, it is her lucidity that makes her different from the other women of her region and class: and in another respect, she already resembles the Thérèse of the novel in being frustrated from experiencing a more complete human love, and in seeing that the vicissitudes of human love prepare the way for another, higher Love. With this situation, the critic finds it easy to show that the heroine is merely a spokesperson for the author. But none of this matters anyway, since there is no action, no occasion for the heroine's free will to be tested in choosing between the allure of sin and that of Grace.[8]

By allowing Thérèse to grow and become less the edifying example of repentance and more a fully realized individual, Mauriac enormously strengthened the thematic heart of the novel. Again, Kushner isolates the issue:

> If Mauriac didn't keep to the simplified perspective of "Conscience," if he wanted, from the beginning to the end, for his heroine to be given up to the anguish, the weight of her thoughts and acts, it is because he wanted to bring into his novel that night of incertitude which is the climate of human life. (95)

This "night of incertitude" is precisely what Mauriac most wanted to explore—though he had not yet realized this when he drafted "Conscience."

It is something of a paradox that Mauriac was only able to make Thérèse into so revealing a self-portrait by freeing her to be entirely different from himself: the male Catholic writer could best sound his own depths by allowing his heroine to be an antireligious, entirely unique individual. In a conversation with Cecil Jenkins, Mauriac explained that creating Thérèse gradually evolved into a kind of self-expression for him:

> *Thérèse Desqueyroux* was indeed the novel of revolt. The story of Thérèse was the whole of my own drama, a protest, a cry. . . . And I could well say, even though I have never contemplated poisoning anyone, that *Thérèse Desqueyroux* was myself.[9]

The "revolt" of the novel operates on at least two fronts. First, it is a revolt against the idea of the family, revealing it as not the nurturing center of the individual's life but instead a claustrophobic, repressive, vindictive social unit. Closing ranks against any threat or scandal, the Desqueyroux family devolves from a smug bourgeois respectability to an active, inhuman cruelty—delegating the worst tasks, in a genteel way, to the domestics. After the "Conscience" draft, the next title Mauriac used for the story was "L'Esprit de famille" (The Spirit of the Family)—so that the idea of the family was now, in his mind, the real subject of the novel. And he explicated the issue in a conversation with his son Claude in 1962:

> In a sense, *Thérèse Desqueyroux* is me. I put into her all the exasperation I felt with a family I could no longer tolerate.[10]

Mauriac's chafing against his family and the repression it represented to him would become more intense over the next few years, culminating in a crisis during 1929–1930, but that discontent and even anguish is powerfully expressed in the story of Thérèse.

Perhaps even more importantly for Mauriac at this stage in his life, the novel also represents a revolt against an even weightier "family," the Catholic Church itself, or at least against some of its spokesmen, those Catholic critics who condemned his novels for their sympathetic depictions of sinners. That sympathy goes further in *Thérèse Desqueyroux* than in any other of his previous works. The only truly worthy character in the book is a nonbeliever and an attempted murderer, and the respectable Christians are in their own way far more "monstrous" than she is. Again, the epigraph from Baudelaire is essential, reminding the reader that such "monsters" as Thérèse were also created by God, and that they were created to be as they are. And when Mauriac concludes his preface by saying how he would have liked Thérèse to end as a saint but feared being condemned for sacrilege, we can sense the pressures, both external and internal, that he was undergoing.

But if *Thérèse Desqueyroux* represents a revolt against family and against conventional notions of piety, in a purely literary sense it is less a revolt than an embracing of tradition. The novel can be seen as Mauriac's own response to, or versions of, two of the most famous works in French literature. No writer, certainly no French writer, could begin a story about a provincial woman suffocating in an unhappy marriage without thinking of Flaubert's *Madame Bovary* (1857). Flaubert's canvas is of course much larger than Mauriac's, with room for a great deal of satire; Mauriac's is more condensed and consistently somber. Many comparisons between the two novels suggest themselves, though—notably the village life in both stories. And while Flaubert, too, famously announced his identification with his heroine, Emma Bovary, one could say that Mauriac's identification is more complete: we always sympathize with Thérèse, and even if we are horrified by some of the things she does and thinks, Mauriac unambiguously presents her as the novel's moral touchstone. If we know Emma Bovary's story, we can sense it hanging always in the background of *Thérèse Desqueyroux*, and we will expect Thérèse to turn to adultery for fulfillment as Emma did—but we find that Thérèse, despite her fleeting attraction to the pompous adolescent Jean Azevedo, is too intelligent for that, or rather too intellectually honest with herself to pretend any happiness might lie in that direction.

A second masterpiece hovering in the background of the novel is Jean Racine's *Phaedra* (1667). Certain references and some details in imagery make for a comparison that would, again, be natural to any reader familiar with the classic drama, and moreover Mauriac was to publish a superb, highly personal biography of Racine in 1928. Racine, like Mauriac, found himself torn between the conflicting demands of God and Mammon, between those of religion and literature, between those of the spirit and the flesh. The character of Phaedra, caught up in an incestuous passion for her stepson Hippolytus, seems on the surface quite unrelated to Thérèse and her situation. But Thérèse too is a creature of profound passion and the need to love—hers, however, is a passion and love without an object. In this respect, her reference to her hunting-obsessed husband as a young Hippolytus is at first darkly comic, and then deeply pathetic. Finally, in both Phaedra and *Thérèse Desqueyroux*, our sympathies are entirely with the criminal woman, and the forces of conventional righteousness are presented as unfeeling and destructive.

But for all its intertextuality, *Thérèse Desqueyroux* is typically Mauriacian, especially in its setting—the countryside outside Bordeaux, the region known as les Landes, a sandy moorlike area dominated by pines, arid and hot in the summers, rainy and cold in the winters. Nearly all of Mauriac's fiction—and all of the best of it—is set here, where he grew up and where he returned frequently throughout his adult life. He spent most of his youthful summers at the family's estate in Saint-Symphorien (the Saint-Clair of the novel). His mature fiction is marked by an unusually powerful use of settings, and this is most masterfully deployed in *Thérèse Desqueyroux*; nearly every critic of the novel has noted how the setting here is so intensely realized as to become virtually a character in its own right. The novel is rich in unforgettable imagery—the eerie howling of the wind in the pines, the winter rain pouring down like a million prison bars, the sun like burning metal. In his nonfiction also, Mauriac often returned to the region and the effects it had on him. In one essay he described how this setting molded him:

> Walking through this immutable landscape, one's train of thought is broken by no sudden color, no strange sound. The exterior world reduces itself as far as possible, effacing and annihilating itself before the interior world. The moor is the servant of the spirit. . . . It was in this disincarnate, unchanging

region that I, still a child, had the presentiment that we here below were born for eternity.[11]

Mauriac took this setting, so spiritually charged for him, and made it into the arena in which his fictional characters attempt to penetrate and understand their own interior worlds.

We see this setting primarily through Thérèse's eyes, of course, so it seems entirely natural, not a literary artifice, that the external world mirrors her internal states—her moods, her sense of impending entrapment. Finding in the external world an equivalent for the subtle modulations of our inner world—this is of course what we ordinarily call poetry, and *Thérèse Desqueyroux* should be appreciated as Mauriac's most intensely poetic work.[12] But there is something even larger at work in Mauriac's manipulation of setting in the novel. Pierre-Henri Simon points out this larger issue in his discussion of *Thérèse Desqueyroux*. He says that Mauriac was not simply deploying an analogy between the inner and outer worlds, but something deeper, something that is at the heart of Mauriac's psychology and even his theology. Simon says that, between the outer and the inner worlds, Mauriac perceived

> not an analogical relation but a necessary link, a vital solidarity, such that the scene and the event, the physical climate and the moral climate are presented as one, each explained by the other, in a totality at once profoundly psychological and intensely poetic. . . . It is not a question of metaphor, but of an intimate complicity being suggested between the domains of the soul and the flesh. . . . And this is by no means a matter of literary technique: rather, it is the profound exigency of an art that, always aiming to depict the drama of the incarnated spirit, tends always toward a rejoining of the soul and the senses. Mauriac well defined himself as "a metaphysician who works in the concrete." In fact his work resides beyond that idealism that imagines the human person as isolated in his interior world, and that realism that shows us as absorbed by, and overcome by, physical things. The person in Mauriac has a soul within a body, or, rather, he carries his body within his soul.[13]

Of course, we are accustomed to seeing things as just the reverse of this: the body is the receptacle of the soul. But the incarnation of the soul, Mauriac suggests, is more complicated than that simple container metaphor suggests. The traditional theologian may wish to preserve an absolute distinction between soul and body, but the novelist, "metaphysician of the concrete," sees how the two act upon each other in mysterious but powerful ways. This truth was explored most deeply, perhaps, by the poet who provides the novel's epigraph: Charles Baudelaire. To choose just one of his poems touching on the subject, his "wretched monk" lamented this aspect of the human condition:

> My soul's a tomb that, wretched cenobite,
> I travel in throughout eternity;
> Nothing adorns the walls of this sad shrine.[14]

The domain of the literary artist—at least of the artist haunted by the idea of the incarnated soul, as were Baudelaire and Mauriac—is not of the spirit or the flesh alone, but the often agonized intersection between the two.

This leads us inevitably to the question of whether and how *Thérèse Desqueyroux* is a Catholic novel, as opposed to simply a novel written by a Catholic. As we have seen, Mauriac looked back on it as a novel of revolt—a revolt against Catholicism itself, or at least against certain aspects of Catholicism that had become as intolerable to Mauriac as marriage had to Thérèse. Certainly, the novel has been widely appreciated by entirely secular readers, among whom are many who would be repelled by any overt Catholicism. And even as informed and searching a reader as Jean Lacouture can say this about the novel:

> It marks . . . the limit, at least the provisional one, of [Mauriac's] removal from Christianity. In none of his books is faith so coldly deserted, in none is the absence of God so oppressive. . . .[15]

Thérèse herself feels this absence of God deeply, true—but does the novel itself depict or suggest a world without God? It goes against the trend of most criticism of the novel to say so, but I believe *Thérèse Desqueyroux* is one of Mauriac's most profoundly Catholic novels—as well as being his most artistically accomplished one. To begin with, Providence is vigorously present in the novel, perhaps most strikingly in some scenes involving the minor character Aunt Clara. The old, deaf sister of Thérèse's father is only tolerated, at best, by the Desqueyroux family. Less than adept at lip-reading, she chatters constantly to avoid having to puzzle out what others are saying. As adolescents, Thérèse and her friend Anne mock her, and later, Bernard's contempt for her is only thinly dissembled. Moreover, Clara offends the pious Desqueyroux sensibilities by her rabid anticlericalism and distrust of religion. But for all this, it is Clara who lives the social imperatives of Christ: she is the one who works tirelessly and unpretentiously for the local poor, seeing to their needs without expecting any reward. And she is the only one in the novel who truly loves Thérèse selflessly and unconditionally, and has done so since Thérèse was a little girl.

Clara makes for an unlikely saint, living entirely outside, and even in opposition to, the church, yet she embodies and acts out the church's most vital teachings. Clara is in fact closer to God—in whom she doesn't much believe—than are the respectable, pharisaical Desqueyroux family who make so grand a show of attending church services regularly. And this connection between Clara and God is brought to an extraordinary climax (even a shocking one, if the reader has been led to expect this to be an entirely realist novel) in chapter X. At that point, Thérèse is in her deepest moment of despair and resolves on suicide; she is pulled back from the act only by the sudden death of Clara. Mauriac shows us in this chapter how deeply and, indeed, spiritually linked Clara is to Thérèse, via her simple love for the young woman. As Bernard lays out the fate he and the family have determined for Thérèse, Clara looks in at the keyhole, then squats alone on the stairs, in the grip of an increasing, vague terror for her beloved niece; she only goes to bed later out of fear of Bernard, and she lies there in the dark, out of breath, her eyes wide open. Her death is discovered at the very moment Thérèse is about to take the poison that will end her life, and the discovery puts an end to all Thérèse's thoughts of suicide. Clara's death is thus presented to us as a substitution for Thérèse's, a case of giving up her life for her niece—it is providential, not coincidental. It is an example of a motif in Catholic literature sometimes called vicarious suffering, and sometimes called mystical substitution. Theodore P. Fraser notes the presence of the motif in earlier writers such as Dostoevsky and Léon Bloy, saying, "in its simplest form this term means the offering of one's life for another, following Christ's example."[16] This motif of substitution has been widely discussed in Mauriac's later novel, *Le Noeud de vipères* (Viper's Tangle), but has received little attention in *Thérèse Desqueyroux*— where it is equally striking and equally important thematically.

Clara's death shows us that the world of *Thérèse Desqueyroux* is one where a spiritual economy allows for the suffering, even the death, of one to pay for the sins of another—a fact that Thérèse herself dimly comprehends at the close of chapter X, though she goes on to reject the intervention as having been mere chance. Clara's presence in the novel demonstrates how the truly Christ-like among us are more likely to be found among the marginalized, the ridiculed, and the rejected than among the conventionally pious. If this theme constitutes a "revolt" against Catholicism, it is a revolt that urges us not to abandon the faith but to return to its real essence, and to reject the false shows of smug righteousness.

Where does Thérèse herself fit within this spiritual economy? She is, formally at least, a nonbeliever. As André Joubert puts it, "The religious hypocrisy of the Desqueyroux family, combined with the anticlericalism of her father and Clara, together deprived her of the circumstances that would be favorable to faith."[17] Yet, Joubert adds, she continues to feel a sense of religious inquietude, manifested in her fascination with the local priest, her often religious vocabulary, and her recurrent concern with the relation between God and His creatures (185). Still, she remains acutely aware of her isolation, and her religious leanings never coalesce into a faith that could help or console her, and she drifts into an anomic state, so dissociated from the reality around her that murdering her husband becomes only a vaguely interesting experiment. She feels no connection even to her daughter—the "fruit of her womb," as she sarcastically expresses it, as if she were a sort of anti-Mary. She is unable to enter into the primary roles a woman of her region and class was expected to play, but far from feeling liberated by this, she often envies the other women who are able to sublimate all their personal and individual desires into being good wives and mothers; and she is always, painfully, aware of her difference and her aloneness.

The "Conscience" draft suggested that repressed lesbianism was at the root of Thérèse's problems, but in the finished novel this is only one thread in a tangled skein of conflicts and motives. Richard Griffiths, however, argues that the lesbianism of "Conscience" remains important in *Thérèse Desqueyroux* and that her sexual frigidity and homosexuality provide the key to her motivation in poisoning Bernard.[18] He quotes a 1927 letter in which Mauriac regrets not having stressed her sexuality sufficiently in the finished novel—which seems conclusive as to Mauriac's intentions with the character. But of course there is often a great gap between what the author intends and what the work itself presents to us. Some other critics, like William Kidd, have suggested that the essence of her conflict can be located in her relation to her father, in a version of the Oedipal complex.[19] Given Mauriac's ambivalence toward, and often hostility to, psychoanalysis (he mocks it in the later short story, "Thérèse at the Doctor's"), it seems unlikely that he consciously employed the Oedipal model, but whether or not one uses Freudian terminology, it is clear that the relation between Thérèse and her father is a troubled one—at least in that he does not fulfill the role of a loving father who helps to give her a sense of her own identity and value.

Shut out from sexual love, from her father's love, and from the fulfillment other women find in their social roles, she yearns above all not to be alone, and her naïve fantasies of simple love during her long agony in the upper room are among the most heartwrenching pages Mauriac ever wrote. Again, we should recall the Baudelaire epigraph to the novel in contemplating Thérèse's character: she too was made by God, and He made her this way—isolated, unable to work her own way out of her suffering. At the end of the powerful chapter XI, Mauriac's own voice enters the text, asking whether it could be that her suffering is not simply an accident but in fact the reason for her existence. She is perhaps marked out for a life of sorrow and rejection—as much as, for example, Jesus Christ was. The suggestion is that she, like Aunt Clara, is in some mysterious way an agent of God's providence, that she has a role to play in the spiritual economy of this world.

And then, surprisingly, at the novel's end she is freed. When Bernard, having abandoned her to the increasingly brutal hands of the domestic Balionte, finally sees her in her emaciated, sickly state, his heart is softened. Love doesn't soften him—Bernard is one of those, Mauriac tells us, without love—but the more primitive emotion of fear does. He recalls an image from childhood of "the Prisoner of Poitiers"—the woman who was imprisoned by her family for twenty-five years, and whose hideous photos were in all the newspapers when Bernard was a child. As a child, Bernard may have felt some pity in contemplating that photo tacked up in the outhouse; as an adult, though, the emotion it triggers is fear—fear of scandal, the worst thing imaginable for his respectable bourgeois family. He imagines himself and his mother having to endure the humiliation and contempt that the Poitiers scandal heaped upon the Bastian family, and it is this rather than pity for the victim that changes him. But this fear, base and self-serving as it is, leads Bernard to some tenderness, as he carefully nurses Thérèse back to health and finally sets her free in Paris. It is true that he does the right thing for the wrong reason, but at least he does do the right thing, and he rises above his worst self in doing it. Again, we have the sense that even Bernard is being guided into playing his part in some larger plan.

Our last view of Thérèse is, to use Mauriac's metaphor, as she plunges into the river of humanity that is Paris. The archetypally isolated woman, intellectually superior to her countryside relatives, now has the chance of having everything in life that she has been so miserably lacking. As she adjusts her makeup, a little tipsy after her wine, she leaves us in a state of near exaltation. Here, she hopes, she will at last fit in and become one of the "living human forest," no longer the solitary one listening to the moaning of the Argelouse pines. For Thérèse—and for the reader who has pitied her and empathized with her—this is in every way a happy ending beyond all expectation. Such an ending comes as something of a shock to us, as the tenor of the rest of the novel has been so bleak and foreboding. And the wish expressed in Mauriac's preface returns to us as we read this ending—that as the author leaves her on the Paris sidewalk, he hopes she is not alone. The words hang over the novel's conclusion like a valediction and a blessing.

It is unfortunate, though, that Mauriac remained fascinated by the character of Thérèse and returned to her several times in later fiction; in that later fiction, the novel's sense of blessing is entirely gone. It is as if Mauriac, after his period of religious and personal crisis and his recommitment to Catholicism,[20] felt compelled to give Thérèse a more conventional moral condemnation. Jean Lacouture refers to these later Thérèse stories as "a sort of *mea culpa* on the part of the novelist" (316). We meet Thérèse again briefly in the novel *What Was Lost*, she is the main character in two short stories ("Thérèse at the Hotel" and "Thérèse at the Doctor's") and in the novel *La Fin de la nuit* (The End of the Night). And in all of these, she is depicted as an unhappy and unrepentant sinner. In *What Was Lost*, she is almost demonic, haunting the streets of nighttime Paris and seeming to want to seduce the innocent young country boy, Alain Forcas. There is an active malevolence about the Thérèse of these later stories that is utterly foreign to the character in *Thérèse Desqueyroux*. The moral judgment in these later works is so overdetermined that Jean-Paul Sartre, after reading *The End of the Night*, was moved to write a crushing attack on Mauriac, calling him a mere moralist and denying him the title of novelist.[21] And even the most vigorous supporter of Mauriac must admit that Sartre was largely right. Mauriac himself became convinced of it, after his initial anger had faded. In 1950, he put it this way:

> If Thérèse, in the first book that bore her name, imposed herself on me, I was the one who imposed himself on her in *The End of the Night*; and it wasn't just chance that Jean-Paul Sartre chose that book to mount the best attack on me.[22]

In these later depictions of the character, Mauriac denied her the freedom that he had allowed her between "Conscience, the Divine Instinct" and *Thérèse Desqueyroux*, and these later works seem like something of a betrayal of his own artistic and theological imperatives. He had been entirely aware of this issue, of course, long before Sartre's attack. In the 1933 essay, "Le Romancier et ses personnages" (The Novelist and His Characters), he stated that characters must be allowed the freedom to become themselves, and the novelist must not seek to turn them into examples or lessons or mouthpieces. The more truly alive a novel's characters are, Mauriac said, the less they will tamely submit to what the novelist wants them to be or do.[23] The later works make their moral points well enough, and they are not without their pleasures for the reader, but they ultimately trivialize the mysterious, profound character we meet in *Thérèse Desqueyroux*.

Of course, one can hardly blame Mauriac for his fascination with the character. Like Emma Bovary, like Phaedra, she is one of those miracles of artistic creation to whom we return again and again, each time feeling that now we understand her at last, but each time feeling that sense of understanding slip away from us ultimately. She is a character who, in Simon's words, carries her body within her soul, and she moves through a landscape that is never merely landscape but somehow intimately linked to both the human and the supernatural. Like Baudelaire's world, the world of *Thérèse Desqueyroux* can seem literally godforsaken, but a more sensitive reading shows us it is a world in which God is intensely and constantly active—as when Thérèse at first sees the pine forests as ominous jailers, but later hears in them the sound of human suffering, and hears in them an innate sympathy.

◆ ◆ ◆

I wish to express my gratitude, first, to Jean Mauriac for his encouragement of this translation. The staff at the Bibliothèque Nationale in Paris were, as always, extremely helpful to me in my research. My specific debts to many other Mauriac scholars are indicated in the notes, but I must record my continual recourse to two magisterial works: Jacques Petit's edition of Mauriac's novels, and Jean Lacouture's biography.

Colleagues and friends who offered advice and encouragement include Don Briel, Rick Holton, Michael Mikolajczak, and David Rathbun. Dr. Richard Kyllo provided me with helpful medical advice regarding the prescriptions forged by Thérèse as well as the symptoms evinced by her husband. A sabbatical leave from my teaching at the University of St. Thomas allowed me the time to complete this translation. And Jeremy Langford at Sheed & Ward again proved himself to be the most supportive of editors.

Finally, I am most indebted to my wife Laraine, who, like me, first fell under the spell of Thérèse Desqueyroux as an undergraduate student. The many conversations she has had with me over the years about Thérèse have been invaluable, and she again gave generously of her time in formatting the final text.

Notes

1. Quoted in Jean Lacouture, *François Mauriac: Le Sondeur d'âbimes, 1885–1933* (Paris: Éditions du Seuil, 1980), p. 220.

2. Nicholas Hewitt, "Mauriac dans le contexte culturel des années vingt: La Tentation de la littérature mondaine," *Nouveaux Cahiers François Mauriac*, 1, 1993, p. 63.

3. Charles Du Bos, *François Mauriac et le problème du romancier catholique* (Paris: Éditions Corrêa, 1933), p. 57.

4. See the discussion of this crisis period in the introduction to *"God and Mammon" and "What Was Lost"* (Sheed & Ward, 2003).

5. Jean Lacouture tells the Canaby story in detail in his biography of Mauriac, pp. 294–297.

6. Mauriac, "Le Romancier et ses personnages" [The Novelist and His Characters], in Jacques Petit, ed., *François Mauriac: Oeuvres romanesques et théâtrales completes* (Paris: Gallimard, 1992), vol. II, p. 844.

7. Mauriac's untitled article was printed in the Portuguese newspaper *Bandarra* on June 8, 1935, and is reproduced in Petit, p. 927.

8. Eva Kushner, *Mauriac* (Paris: Desclée De Brouwer, 1972), p. 95.

9. Cecil Jenkins, *Mauriac* (New York: Barnes and Noble, 1965), p. 75.

10. Quoted in Lacouture, p. 321.

11. Mauriac, "Spiritualité des Landes" [1936], quoted in Théodore Quoniam, *François Mauriac: Du Péché à la rédemption* (Paris: Tequi, 1984), pp. 46–47.

12. Many critics have conferred the term "poetic" on Mauriac's fiction, often using the term in a more general way to denote that his prose is

intense, or evocative. These various uses of the term are surveyed by Bernard Swift in "Espace fictive, espace poétique?" in *Nouveaux Cahiers François Mauriac*, 8, 2000, pp. 137–145.

13. Pierre-Henri Simon, *Mauriac par lui-même* (Paris: Editions du Seuil, 1963), p. 38.

14. Charles Baudelaire, "The Wretched Monk" ["Le Mauvais moine"], in *The Flowers of Evil* [1857], trans. James McGowan (London: Oxford University Press, 1993), p. 29.

15. Lacouture, p. 307.

16. Theodore P. Fraser, *The Modern Catholic Novel in Europe* (New York: Twayne, 1994), p. xv.

17. André Joubert, "La Tragédie spirituelle de Thérèse Desqueyroux," in André Seailles, ed., *Mauriac devant le problème du mal* (Paris: Klincksieck, 1994), p. 183.

18. Richard Griffiths, *Le Singe de Dieu: François Mauriac entre le 'roman catholique' et la littérature contemporaine, 1913–1930* (Paris: L'Esprit du Temps, 1996), pp. 118–121.

19. William Kidd, "Oedipal and pre-Oedipal Elements in *Thérèse Desqueyroux*" in John E. Flower and Bernard C. Swift, eds., *François Mauriac: Visions and Reappraisals* (Oxford: Berg, 1989), pp. 25–45.

20. On Mauriac's period of crisis and its resolution, see the introduction to *"God and Mammon" and "What Was Lost."*

21. Jean-Paul Sartre, "François Mauriac and Freedom," in *Literary Essays*, trans. Annette Michelson (New York: Philosophical Library, 1957), pp. 7–23.

22. Lacouture, p. 307.

23. "Le Romancier et ses personnages," p. 850.

Thérèse Desqueyroux

Lord, have pity, have pity on the mad men and women! O Creator! Can those monsters exist in the eyes of The One who knows why they exist, how they created themselves, and how they could not have made themselves any other way.'

Charles Baudelaire

Thérèse, there are many who will say that you don't exist. But I know that you do, I who for many years have caught sight of you, I who have often stopped you in your passing by, I who now unmask you.

As an adolescent, I remember having seen you in a suffocating courtroom, surrounded by lawyers less ferocious than the plumed women observing the trial, with your small, pale face and your thin lips.

Later, in a country living room, you appeared to me in the guise of a haggard young wife, irritated by the fussing care of aged relatives and a naïve husband. "What's wrong with her?" they were saying. "We give her everything she could possibly want."

And since then, I've often wondered at your high, beautiful forehead, your hand just a little too large. Often, I've seen you in that living cage that is a family, pacing like a she-wolf, and I've seen your sad and malevolent eye fixed on me.

Many will be surprised that I've been able to imagine a creature even more hateful than all the characters in my other novels. They will wonder why I don't depict the sort of character who bristles with virtue and who wears his heart on his sleeve. But those with "hearts on their sleeves" don't have a story. But those hearts that are buried, the ones deeply intermingled with the mud of the flesh—those hearts are the ones I know.

I would have liked it, Thérèse, if your sorrow had led you to God; and I have long wished that you had been worthy of the name of Saint Locusta.[2] But many would have cried out "Sacrilege!" if I had depicted you that way—including some who believe in the Fall and the redemption of our tortured souls.

But at least I retain the hope that you, on the sidewalk where I have abandoned you, are not alone.

I

The lawyer opened a door. Standing in the obscure courthouse corridor, Thérèse Desqueyroux felt the fog on her face, and she breathed it in deeply. She hesitated, afraid of who might be waiting for her. A man with his collar turned up emerged from under a plane tree; she saw it was her father. The lawyer called out, "Insufficient cause," and turned to Thérèse:

"You can go out: there's nobody here."

She descended the wet steps. Yes, the little square seemed deserted. Her father didn't embrace her, nor even look at her; he was asking questions of Duros, the lawyer, who replied in a low voice, as if someone might be watching them. She heard them only confusedly.

"I'll get the official notice of insufficient cause tomorrow."

"There won't be any surprises?"

"No. The game is over, as they say."

"After my son-in-law's testimony, it was all settled."

"Settled—well—you never know."

"Once he spoke up and admitted he never counted the drops . . ."

"You know, Larroque, in these sorts of cases, the testimony of the victim . . ."

Thérèse raised her voice: "There was no victim."

"I meant to say, victim of his own imprudence, Madame."

Now the two men looked at the young woman—standing motionless, wrapped tightly in her raincoat—at her pale, expressionless face. She asked where the coach was; her father had ordered it left outside of town, on the road to Budos, so as not to attract attention.

They walked across the square. Leaves from the plane trees were stuck to the benches wet with rain. Fortunately, the days had been getting shorter. And, to get to the Budos road, they could take streets that were among the most deserted ones in the county. Thérèse walked between the two men, who again began conversing as if she weren't there; instead, as if inconvenienced by this woman walking between them, they jostled her with their elbows. So she began to walk a little behind them, removing her left glove to run her hand along the moss on the old stone walls. Now and then, a laborer on a bicycle or an old cart passed them; the spurting mud obliged her to stay close to the wall. But the dusk concealed Thérèse, preventing people from recognizing her. These smells, of a bakery, of the fog, were no longer simply the odors of evening in a small town: now they were the scent of life itself, the life that had been given back to her. She closed her eyes and breathed in the sleeping earth, grassy and damp, forcing herself to ignore what the man with the short legs was saying without ever once turning toward his daughter: she could have fallen into a hole, and neither he nor Duros would have noticed. Now they no longer feared to raise their voices.

"The testimony of Monsieur Desqueyroux was excellent, yes. But he had this prescription: in short, it's a matter of a forgery. And it was Doctor Pedemay who brought the complaint . . ."

"He's retracted it."

"Still, the explanation he gave—this unknown person who brought the prescription to him . . ."

Thérèse, less out of fatigue than the need to escape the talk that had been deafening her for weeks, slowed her walk even more, but it was useless: she couldn't help hearing her father's falsetto:

"I told her often enough: 'Poor girl, do better than that; do better than that.'"

He had indeed said it often enough, and he had done everything right. Why was he still upset? What they call the honor of the family name is safe; when the elections come around, no one will remember this story at all. So Thérèse thought, wishing she didn't have to rejoin the two men. But in the heat of their discussion, they had stopped in the middle of the road and were gesturing at each other.

"Listen, Larroque, go on the offensive in the Sunday *Gleaner*—or would you rather I do it? We need a headline, something like 'An Infamous Rumor' . . ."

"No, no, my friend: what would I be responding to, anyway? It's perfectly evident that the whole case was slapped together; they didn't even get handwriting experts. No—silence, concealment—that's the best. I'll do what I must, I'll meet the price, but for the family, we have to cover all that up—cover it all up . . ."

Thérèse didn't hear Duros's reply, because they had walked on ahead. She breathed in the rainy night, as if she were in danger of suffocation, and suddenly she imagined the face of Julie Ballade, the face she had never seen of the grandmother she had never known. The search had been in vain, both at Larroque's and at Desqueyroux's, for a photograph, a daguerreotype, a portrait of this mysterious woman; nothing was known of her, except that one day she had left. Thérèse imagined that she too could be erased one day, annihilated, and that later on they would keep her daughter, little Marie, from ever seeing the image of the woman who had brought her into the world. Right now, Marie would be asleep in a room in the Argelouse house, where Thérèse would arrive later tonight; then she would stand in the darkness and listen to the child sleep; she would bend down and seek out that sleeping life with her lips, as if she were seeking water.

Beside a ditch, the lanterns on a coach with its top closed illuminated two skinny horses. Beyond, from left to right across the road stood up a somber wall of forest. From one side to the other, the tops of the first pines seemed to join in an arc, under which the road mysteriously wound ahead. The sky moved above her, a bed covered with branches. The driver gazed at Thérèse with an air of greedy fascination. When she asked if they would arrive at the Nizan station in time for the last train, he reassured her. Still, it would be best not to delay.

"This is the last time I'll be giving you this chore, Gardere."

"Madame has no further business here?"

She shook her head, as he continued to devour her with his eyes. Would she be stared at like this all her life?

"So, you're all right?" Her father seemed finally to have noticed she was there. Thérèse looked quickly at the bilious face, the cheeks with the rough beard, yellowish white in the bright glare of the lanterns. She said quietly, "I've suffered so much . . . I feel broken down . . ." and then interrupted herself: what's the point of talking? He isn't listening; he doesn't even see her anymore. Why would he care what she feels? The only thing that matters is his interrupted ascent to the Senate, compromised by this daughter (and they're all hysterics, when they aren't idiots). Happily, she was no longer a Larroque; she was a Desqueyroux. The scandal of a trial averted, he could breathe again. Now, how to prevent his adversaries from twisting the knife? Tomorrow, he would go to see the prefect. Thanks be to God, he controlled the editor of the *Conservator*: that story about the girls . . . He took Thérèse's arm.

"Get in now. It's time."

Then the lawyer, out of either malice or a sense that he shouldn't let Thérèse go without saying something to her, asked if she would be rejoining Monsieur Bernard Desqueyroux tonight. She replied, "Of course; my husband's waiting for me," but in saying it she realized for the first time since leaving the judge that, in fact, within a few hours, she would actually cross the threshold of the room where her husband lay, still somewhat ill, and that an indefinite sequence of days and nights would open up, and that she would have to live through all of them beside that man.

She had often made exactly the same journey that she was about to take, while she was living with her father on the little town's outskirts, since the beginning of the case. But then, she had had nothing to think about but exactly what she was supposed to tell her husband; before getting in the carriage, she would listen to Duros's last instructions as to the responses Monsieur Desqueyroux should make at the next interrogation. And in those days, Thérèse felt no anxiety, no discomfort at the idea of finding herself face to face with the sick man. The issue between them was only what one must say or not say, not what had really happened. The couple had never been so well united as during the preparation of the defense, two united in one body—the body of their little girl, Marie. For the judge's consumption, they concocted a simple story, tightly organized, satisfying to the most rigorously logical mind. In those days, Thérèse had climbed up into this same coach—but with what impatience then to get the journey over with, whereas tonight she wished it would never reach its goal. She remembered how then, barely seated in the coach, she had wanted already to be in the room at Argelouse, and she would run over in her memory the instructions for Bernard Desqueyroux—that he shouldn't be afraid to affirm that she had spoken to him one night about this prescription that an unknown man had asked her to get for him, on the pretext that he dared not approach the pharmacist himself, as he owed him money . . . But Duros didn't think Bernard would go so far as to pretend to have admonished his wife for such an imprudent agreement . . .

Now that the nightmare had dissipated, what would Bernard and Thérèse talk about tonight? She visualized the desolate house where he awaited her; she pictured the bed in the middle of the tiled room, the low lamp on the table, among newspapers and prescription bottles . . . The watchdogs, awakened by the coach, would bay and then quiet down, and the silence would take over, as it did during those nights when she watched Bernard wracked with hideous vomiting. She forced herself to imagine the first glances they would exchange; then the night, and the next day, and the day after that, the weeks ahead in the Argelouse house, when they would no longer have to work on a story together about the drama they had been through. There would be nothing else between them except what had really—what had really . . . Clutched by panic, Thérèse stammered, turning toward the lawyer, but actually addressing the old man:

"I plan to stay with Monsieur Desqueyroux a few days. Then, if things are going well, I'll return to my father's."

"Oh! No, no, my dear!"

And as Gardere shifted on his seat, Monsieur Larroque said more quietly: "Have you gone completely mad? Leave your husband at such a time? You must be like two fingers on one hand— like two fingers on one hand, do you understand? Until death . . ."

"You're right, father; what was I thinking? But then, you'll be coming to Argelouse?"

"Thérèse, no; I'll expect you on market Thursdays, as usual. You'll go on just as you always have!"

It was incredible that she couldn't see how the slightest deviation from their routine could be fatal. Was this clear? Could he count on Thérèse? She had caused her family enough misery . . .

"You'll do everything your husband tells you to do. I can't give you any better advice than that."

And he pushed her into the coach.

Thérèse saw the lawyer extend his hand toward her, with its hard, dirty nails. "All's well that ends well," he said, and he meant it from the bottom of his heart, because if the case had gone to trial he wouldn't have made his fee: the family would have turned to Peyrecave, the Bordeaux attorney.[3] Yes, all was well . . .

T hérèse liked it, the musty smell of leather in these old coaches. She consoled herself for having forgotten her cigarettes by reminding herself she disliked smoking in the dark. The lanterns illuminated the banks, the clusters of ferns, the trunks of the giant pines. The carriage's shadow took strange shapes against the piles of stones by the side of the road as they passed. Sometimes a cart would pass, the mules hewing off to the right without the sleeping driver having to budge. Thérèse thought they might never get to Argelouse. Over an hour by coach to the Nizan train station, and then the little train that stopped at every station along the way. Then Saint-Clair itself, where she would get off, and then ten kilometers by the trap to Argelouse (the road is such that no automobile would dare take it at night). At any point, fate might step forward and deliver her. Thérèse gave in to the imagination that had possessed her the night before the judgment, when the case might still have gone forward: she waited for the earth to tremble. Removing her hat, she settled her small, pale head against the musty leather, surrendering her body to the carriage's jolts. Until tonight, hers had been a life of being hunted; now, she was safe, and now she became aware of her utter exhaustion. The sunken cheeks, the high cheekbones, the parted lips, and the superb broad forehead—an image of one of the damned, yes, though people had not recognized her guilt—damned to eternal solitude. That charm of hers that people had called irresistible was the charm of one whose face revealed a hidden torment, the shooting pain of an interior wound—of one, at least, who hadn't found a way to conceal it. Now, jolting along in this coach, on this road like a trail through the thick obscurity of the pines, her mask removed, the young woman gently caressed her burning face with her right hand. What would be the first words from Bernard, whose false testimony had saved her? Probably he would ask her nothing tonight—but tomorrow? Thérèse closed her eyes, opened them again, and sensing the horses pulling harder, forced herself to remember this particular rise in the road. Ah— don't try to predict. Maybe tomorrow will be simpler than it seems. Don't try to predict. Sleep. Why was she out of the coach? That man standing before the green baize desk—the examining magistrate—him again. He knows it's all been arranged. He shakes his head, left to right: he can't declare insufficient cause because a new fact has just come to light. A new fact? Thérèse turned so the enemy would not see her anxiety. "Remember now, Madame. In the inner pocket of that old cape of yours—the one you only wore in October, in hunting season—have you perhaps forgotten something, lied about something?" Impossible to deny it—impossible to breathe. Keeping his eyes fixed on his trapped prey, the judge places a tiny package on the table, sealed in red. Thérèse could recite the prescription from memory, as the judge read it from the envelope in a cutting tone:

Chloroform: 30 grams
Aconite grains: 20
Digitalis: 20 grams

The judge burst into laughter. The brake shrieked against the wheel. Thérèse woke up: she breathed in, filling her lungs with the fog—this must be the slope by the stream. She had dreamed like this as an adolescent when she had made some error in school, forcing her to go back and redo all her work. Tonight, she felt the same sense of commitment to the process as she had in those student nights: only a little hurdle to go now, because the decree of insufficient cause was not yet official. "But you know the attorney must be notified . . ."

✦ ✦ ✦

Chapter II

Free—what more could she want? It would be easy to ）
way to make life with Bernard possible. Open herself up to him
the way, keep nothing back: that's the way to deliverance. Every
thing that had been hidden would come to the light, starting tonight.
The resolution lifted Thérèse up in a kind of joy. Before reaching
Argelouse, she would have time to "prepare her confession," the
phrase dear Anne de la Trave used every Saturday during those
happy vacation times. Little sister Anne, dear innocent, what a
place you have in this story! The purest people have no idea what
they're mixing with every day, every night, what poisonous things
their little childlike feet are stepping across.

She was right, certainly, that girl, when she said to the rational,
mocking high-schooler Thérèse: "You can't imagine the feeling of
freedom after confession and absolution—when everything's
cleared away and you can start your life over again." All Thérèse
now had to do was make the resolution to confess everything in
order to feel a delicious sense of things loosening around her: "Bernard will know everything; I'll tell him . . ."

What would she tell him? Where would she start? Would words
be able to express her confused tangle of desires, resolutions,
unplanned acts? How did they do it, those people who really knew
the crimes they were committing? "But I don't know my crimes. I
never wanted to do what I'm charged with. I don't even know what
I did want. That mad power I felt inside me, around me, I never
knew what it was or where it was taking me—it took its own way,
destroying as it went, and I myself was terrified of it . . ."

♦ ♦ ♦

A smoky glass lantern illuminated the old wall of the Nizan station, and the parked carriage—but how quickly the shadows re-
formed themselves just beyond the light! From the train parked at
the platform came animal roars, and then sad, bleating sounds. Gardere took Thérèse's bag, and again seemed to devour her with his
eyes. His wife must have given him orders: "Look her over good,
see how she looks, how she carries herself . . ." For Larroque's
coachman, she summoned up that smile of hers that made people
say, "You don't really ask whether she's pretty or ugly; you just
submit to that charm." She asked him to go to the ticket window for

her, because she feared having to cross the waiting room, where two farm wives sat, knitting, baskets on their knees, their heads nodding.

When he brought out the ticket, she told him to keep the change. He touched his cap to her, grasped the reins, and turned one last time to stare at his employer's daughter.

The train wasn't ready yet. In the past, during the long vacations, or on the days of returning to classes, Thérèse Larroque and Anne de la Trave loved this stop at the Nizan station. They ate fried eggs and ham at the inn, then walked off, arms around each other's waist, down this road, so dark tonight. But in those long-gone days, Thérèse never saw anything but the whiteness of the moon. They laughed at their long shadows, intertwined behind them. They must have talked about their teachers, their friends—the one defending her convent school, the other her lycée. "Anne . . ." Thérèse spoke her name aloud in the darkness. Anne was the first thing she would have to tell Bernard about. Bernard, the most precise of men: he classified all the feelings, separating them off from each other, unaware of the complex network of passages through which they were joined together. How could she coax him into the indeterminate regions where Thérèse had lived and suffered? But it had to be done. The only thing possible now was to go into his room, sit beside his bed, and lead him stage by stage to the point where he would interrupt her: "I understand now. Get up; I forgive you."

She walked quietly through the stationmaster's garden, smelling the chrysanthemums without seeing them. No one was in the firstclass compartment, and at any rate the light would be too dim to reveal her face there. Impossible to read—but what story could be anything but dull to Thérèse, compared with that of her own, terrible life? She might die of shame, of anguish, of remorse, of exhaustion—but she would not die of boredom.

She seated herself in a corner and closed her eyes. Surely a woman of her intelligence could think of a way to make this drama intelligible? Yes, after her confession, Bernard would raise her up: "Go in peace, Thérèse, and worry no more. Here in this Argelouse house, you and I will await death together, without ever sorting out all the things that have happened. I'm thirsty. Go down to the kitchen. Fix me a glass of orangeade. I'll drink it all off at one gulp, even if it's cloudy. What does it matter if the taste reminds me of the morning hot chocolate from those days? Do you recall, my beloved, my vomiting? Your dear hand supported my head; you didn't recoil from the greenish liquid, and my fainting didn't frighten you. But how pale you looked that night when I realized I couldn't feel my arms or legs. I trembled, do you remember? And that fool Doctor Pedemay was dumbfounded that my pulse was so high, my temperature so low . . ."

"Ah," Thérèse thought, "he won't have understood. I'll have to start all over again from the beginning . . ." But where is it, the beginning of our acts? Our life, when we want to grasp it whole, is like those plants you can never pull out of the soil with all their roots. Should Thérèse go back and start with her childhood? But even childhood is an ending of sorts, a culmination.

♦ ♦ ♦

Thérèse's childhood: from the snow at its source, the muddiest river. At school, she appeared indifferent to or absent from all the little tragedies that befell her friends. The teachers often used Thérèse Larroque as an example for the others: "Thérèse asks only for the happiness that comes from knowing she is of a superior human type. Her own conscience is the only light she needs. Her pride in belonging to the human elite sustains her better than any fear of punishment." So one of the teachers put it. Thérèse asked herself, "Was I so happy? Was I so candid? Everything before my marriage now seems to have taken on an aura of purity—by way of contrast, of course, with the ineradicable dirtying of the marriage. School back then, before I became a wife and mother, seems like a paradise. But then I wasn't aware of it. How could I know, during those prelife years, how I would come to live my real life? I *was* pure—an angel, yes! But an angel full of passions. Whatever my teachers thought or said, I suffered, and I made others suffer. I took joy in the evil I caused, and even in that done to me by my friends, a pure suffering untouched by any remorse: sorrows and joys born from the most innocent pleasures."

All Thérèse wanted, in the hot season, was to be judged worthy of Anne, who she would meet beneath the oaks of Argelouse. She needed to be able to say to the Sacré-Coeur child, "To be as pure as you, I don't need all those ribbons and bows, all those clichés . . ." For Anne de la Trave's purity was composed mostly of ignorance. The sisters at Sacré-Coeur interposed a thousand misty veils between reality and their girls. Thérèse felt contempt for the way they confounded purity and ignorance. "You, darling, you don't know life," she would say in those far-off Argelouse summers. Those beautiful summers . . . Seated now in the little train that was finally getting under way, Thérèse realized that she had to go back and start with those summers if she wanted to think clearly. Unbelievable but true, that in those dawns, the purest and sweetest of our lives, the worst of storms were already gathering and waiting. Those too-blue mornings—a bad sign for the afternoon and evening weather. They were foreshadowings, annunciations of ravaged flower beds to come, broken branches, and so much mud. Thérèse had never been reflective, had never premeditated at all in her life. There had been no abrupt change, no sudden turning point: she had descended an easy slope, slowly at first, then more quickly. Tonight's lost woman was indeed the young, radiant being of those summers at Argelouse—where she was now returning, furtive and protected by the night.

How tired she was! What's the good of seeking out the hidden causes of what's already been done? The young woman could see nothing outside the windows, only her own dead reflection. The rhythm of the little train changed; the engine gave a long sigh, as it prudently approached a station. An arm holding a lantern, the local patois being shouted out, the anguished squeal of piglets being loaded off: Uzeste already. One station left, and that will be Saint-Clair, where she would have to leave the train and take the trap the rest of the way to Argelouse. So little time remained for Thérèse to prepare her defense!

III

A rgelouse is truly a "land's end," one of those places beyond
which there's nowhere to go. Less than a village, it is what
people in this region call a *quartier*; it is a hamlet with a few ten-
anted farms scattered around a rye field, without a church or town
hall or even cemetery, ten kilometers from the village of Saint-
Clair, to which it's connected by a single dirt road. Full of ruts and
holes, the road degenerates after Argelouse into sandy pathways,
and all the way to the ocean there is nothing but twenty-five kilometers of marshes, lagoons, and spindly pines, lands where at winter's end the sheep are the color of ashes. The best families of Saint-
Clair originated in this area. Around the middle of the last century,
when resin and lumber began to add to the meager incomes they
derived from their flocks, the grandparents of today's families
moved to Saint-Clair, and their Argelouse homes became tenant
farms. Awnings with sculpted supports or the occasional marble
chimney testify to the places' ancient dignity. With every year, they
shrink down a little more, and the sinking, tired wing of a great roof
almost comes to touch the ground.

Two of these old places, however, are still inhabited by their
owners. The Larroque and Desqueyroux families maintained their
houses in the condition in which they had inherited them. Jerome
Larroque, mayor and council member of Bazas, had his principal
residence in the town, but he wanted to maintain the Argelouse
house, which had come to him through his wife; she had died during childbirth when Thérèse was still in the cradle. He was not sur-

prised that his daughter liked spending her vacations there. She would move there in July, under the guardianship of his father's elder sister, Aunt Clara; old and deaf, she also loved the solitude here because, as she said, she didn't have to pay attention to people's lips moving, and anyway all there was to hear out here was the wind in the pines. Larroque was doubly pleased with Argelouse, as it not only got his daughter off his hands every year but also brought her together with Bernard Desqueyroux, the man she would marry one day, in accord with the wishes of both families—though the engagement was not official.

Bernard Desqueyroux had inherited from his father a house next to Larroque's; once hunting season began, nobody laid eyes on him, and he only came home to sleep in October, having built his hunting cabin nearby. In winter, this highly sensible young man pursued law studies in Paris; in the summer, he spent as few days as he could with his family. He was exasperated with Victor de la Trave, the man his widowed mother had married "without a red cent," a man legendary in Saint-Clair for his spending habits. As for his half-sister Anne, she seemed to Bernard to be too young to be worthy of his attention. Did he give any more thought to Thérèse? Everyone else already had the two of them married, because their properties seemed designed to be merged, and on this point the young man agreed with everyone. But he left nothing to chance, and he took pride in his well-organized life: "Bad luck only comes to those who've earned it," the somewhat too-plump young man liked to say. Up until his marriage, his life was equal parts work and pleasure, and though he disdained neither food nor alcohol nor, above all, hunting, he "worked himself to the bone," his mother said. For after all, a husband must be better educated than his wife, and Thérèse's intelligence was celebrated. A spirited young woman, no doubt, but Bernard knew how to make women yield; and besides, as his mother said, it was a good thing "to have a foot in both camps"—that is, Thérèse's father might be of use to him. At twenty-six, Bernard Desqueyroux—after several "studiously planned" trips to Italy, to Spain, to the Low Countries—would marry the richest and smartest girl in the region, though maybe not the prettiest—but then, "you don't ask whether she's pretty or ugly; you just submit to her charm."

♦ ♦ ♦

Such was the caricature of Bernard that Thérèse drew, and she smiled at it. "But to tell the truth, he was more refined than most of the boys I could have married." The women of the region are greatly superior to the men who, after school, no longer cultivate themselves; their hearts are in the land, and they continue to live there at least in spirit. Nothing matters for them except the pleasures of the land. It would be a betrayal, a personal loss, if they ceased resembling the farmers, gave up the patois and the rough country manners. But under Bernard's hard shell, wasn't there a kind of goodness? When he was close to dying, the farmers said, "There'll never be another gentleman here, after him." Yes, there was goodness, and also a strength of spirit, and a genuine good faith; he rarely spoke of things he didn't know about; he accepted his limitations. As an adolescent, he wasn't at all bad looking, this unpolished Hippolytus—less interested in girls than in the hares he hunted across the fields . . .'

♦ ♦ ♦

However, he wasn't the one whom Thérèse saw—her eyes closed, her head leaning against the window of the coach—it wasn't Bernard who burst toward her on a bicycle in those long-ago mornings around nine, on the road between Argelouse and Saint-Clair, before the heat of the day reached its peak—not the indifferent fiancé, but his little sister Anne, her face glowing. And already the cicadas were awakening from pine to pine, and below the great sky, the furnace of the land began to throb. Flies by the millions rose into the higher branches. "Put your shawl on before you come into the living room: it's glacial in here . . ." And Aunt Clara added, "Have a drink when you've stopped sweating, little one." Anne pointlessly shouted out words of greeting to the deaf woman:

"Don't strain your voice, dear; she can read your lips . . ." But the girl went on in vain, overarticulating every word, deforming her tiny mouth into grimaces; so the puzzled aunt was forced to reply at random, until the two friends had to flee the room in order to be able to laugh freely.

In the corner of the dark coach, Thérèse looked back on those days, the pure days of her life—pure, yet lit by a vague and weak sense of happiness; back then, she didn't know that this troubled light playing upon her joy was to be all she would have in life. Nothing warned her that the sum of her happiness was here in the shadowy living room in the heart of the implacable summer—on the red rep couch, next to Anne, whose closed knees supported a photo album. Where did this happiness come from? Did Anne share even one of Thérèse's interests? She hated reading; she only liked sewing, chattering, and laughing. She had no ideas about anything, whereas Thérèse devoured, indiscriminately, novels by Paul de Kock, the *Causeries de lundi*, the *History of the Consulat*, all the books one finds lying around a country house.[5] They had no pleasures in common, except that of being together in afternoons when the fiery sky laid siege to people barricaded in their semidarkness. Sometimes Anne would get up to see if the heat had broken. But the shutters barely opened, the sun burst in like molten metal, as if it would set fire to the carpets, and everything had to be closed up again.

Even at dusk, when the sun only lit up the bases of the pines, and when a last cicada close to the earth kept its song going, the heat remained, stagnant under the oak trees. As if they were on the shores of a lake, the two friends stretched out on the edge of the rye field. Storm clouds suggested shifting shapes to them, but before Thérèse could make out the winged woman that Anne saw in the sky, it had become, her young friend said, only a strange kind of distended animal.

In September, they could walk out after dinner and wander in the thirsting countryside: Argelouse had not the smallest trickle of water; they had to walk for a long time across the sand before coming to the sources of the river called La Hure. These sources were numerous, bursting out of the thin prairie lands, between the alder roots. The girls' bare feet grew numb in the glacial waters, then quickly dried, then quickly began to burn again. One of the cabins used by the woodcock hunters in October became their refuge, as the living room had. There was nothing to say; no words were necessary: the minutes fled by in those long, innocent rest periods, and the girls never dreamed of moving, no more than the hunter does when he hears the flock approaching and makes the sign for silence. It seemed to them that any movement, even a gesture, would cause this unshaped, chaste happiness to flee. Anne was the first to stretch, impatient to be killing larks at dusk. Thérèse hated this game, but followed her nonetheless, insatiable for her presence. Back in the vestibule, Anne took down the 24-caliber gun that had no recoil. Her friend, remaining seated on the little rise, saw her in the middle of the rye field aiming at the sun as if she would shoot it out. Thérèse covered her ears; a wild cry shot through the air, and the huntress gathered up the wounded bird, gripping it with a careful hand and, while caressing its feathers with her lips, strangled it.

"Are you coming tomorrow?"

"Oh—no, not every day."

She didn't want to see her every day; there was no way to argue with so rational a phrase. Any protest would have seemed, even to Thérèse, incomprehensible. Anne preferred not to come back; she could have, of course, but why come around every day? She said they'd end up being sick of each other. Thérèse replied, "Yes, yes . . . Don't make it a duty. Come back when you feel like it, when there's nothing better to do." The teenage girl on her bicycle disappeared down the already darkening road, ringing her bell.

Thérèse went back toward the house, the farmers waving to her from afar; the children didn't approach her. It was the hour when the sheep flocks gathered under the oaks and would suddenly begin running all together, and the shepherd would cry out. Her aunt waited for her in the doorway, and, as the deaf will do, chattered incessantly so that Thérèse would not speak to her. What was this anguish? She didn't feel like reading; she didn't feel like doing anything. She wandered off again: "Don't go too far; supper's almost ready." She went back to the side of the road, empty now as far as her eye could reach. The clock in the kitchen chimed. Perhaps tonight they would have to light the lamps. The silence was no more profound for the deaf woman, her hands joined on the table-cloth, than it was for the girl with the somewhat emaciated face.

✦ ✦ ✦

Bernard, Bernard, how can I let you into this confused world of mine, you who belong to the race of the blind, the implacably simple race? "But," Thérèse thought, "he'll interrupt my very first words: 'Why did you marry me? I didn't pursue you . . .'" Why had she married him? It was true that he hadn't shown any haste. Thérèse recalled that Bernard's mother, Madame Victor de la Trave, constantly repeated, "He'd have been willing to wait, but she wanted it, she wanted it, she wanted it. She's not one of our kind, unfortunately; for example, she smokes like a chimney—an affectation of hers. But she's very straightforward, as open as can be. We're going to help prod her toward some healthier ideas about things. Of course, not everything about the marriage was perfect. That grandmother Ballade—yes, I know all about it—but that's all forgotten, isn't it? You could scarcely say there'd been a scandal, it was hushed up so completely. Do you believe in heredity? The father has some questionable ideas, but he always gave her only the best examples—he's a lay saint. And he has a long arm. You need everybody's help in this life. And anyway, you have to pass over some things. And, believe it or not, she has more money than we do. Hard to believe, but it's true. And she adores Bernard, into the bargain."

Yes, she had adored him—and no pose or attitude had ever cost her less effort. In the Argelouse living room, or under the oaks by the field's edge, she only had to raise her eyes up to him—her science, her method of representing amorous candor. Such a prey lying at his feet flattered the boy, but didn't surprise him. "Don't play around with her," his mother warned; "she's the type who frets."

✦ ✦ ✦

"I married him because . . ." Her brows knit togeth[...]
her eyes, Thérèse scanned her memory. There was a c[...]
becoming Anne's sister through the marriage. But it w[...]
got the most pleasure out of the idea; the connection [...]
that much to Thérèse. Why be embarrassed to admit it? [...] ...[...]
indifferent to Bernard's two thousand acres. "She always had property in her blood." After long dinners, the table cleared and alcohol
served, Thérèse often stayed on among the men, intrigued by their
conversations about the farms, the mines, the resin, the turpentine.
Appraisals of property fascinated her. No doubt she had been
seduced by the prospect of having dominion over so grand an
extent of forest. "And anyway, he too; he was in love with my pine
trees . . ." But Thérèse may have been obeying a more obscure feeling than what she had so far been able to bring to light. Perhaps she
was seeking less a dominion or a possession out of this marriage
than a refuge. What finally pushed her into it, after all—wasn't it a
kind of panic? A practical girl, a child housewife, she was in a
hurry to take up her station in life, to find her definitive place; she
wanted assurance against some peril that she could not name. She
was never so rational and determined as she had been during the
engagement period; she embedded herself in the family bloc, "she
settled down," she entered into an order of life. She saved herself.

During the spring of their engagement, they took the sandy path
from Argelouse to Vilmeja. Dead leaves on the oak trees overhead
still marred the azure sky; dry ferns from last year were scattered
around on the ground, through which some new, acid green growth
was beginning to pierce. Bernard said, "Be careful with your cigarette. This could still burn; there's no water in the soil." She had
asked, "Is it true that the ferns contain prussic acid?" Bernard didn't
know if they contained enough to be poisonous. He asked her ten-
derly, "Why? Are you interested in dying?" She had laughed. He
had avowed that she was finally becoming simpler. Thérèse remembered that she had closed her eyes, and two strong hands caressed
her face, as a voice said into her ear, "But there are still some fool-
ish ideas in there." She had replied, "For you to drive out, Bernard."
They had watched some masons at work building a room adjoining
a farmhouse in Vilmeja. The owners, from Bordeaux, wanted their
son to move in there, "for his lungs' sake." The sister had died from

the same malady. Bernard felt nothing but disdain for the Azevedo family: "They swear to God they're not Jewish, but you only have to look at them. And along with that, tuberculosis—all these diseases." Thérèse was calm. Anne returned from the St. Sebastian convent school for the wedding. In the wedding party, she would be paired with the Deguilhem boy. She had asked Thérèse to describe for her, "by return post," the dresses the maids of honor would be wearing. "Could you send patterns? It would be best for everybody if we chose matching colors . . ." Thérèse had never known such peace—or rather, what she took to be peace, and what was in fact a halfsleep, the torpor of the reptile within its skin.

IV

The suffocating wedding day in the narrow Saint-Clair church, where the women's cackling drowned out the wheezing harmonium, and the body odor overpowered the incense—this was the day when Thérèse realized she was lost. She had entered the cage like a sleepwalker and, as the heavy door groaned shut, the miserable child in her reawakened. Nothing had changed, but she had the sensation that she would never again be able to be alone. In the thick of a family, she would smolder, like a hidden fire that leaps up onto a branch, lights up a pine tree, then another, then step by step creates a whole forest of torches. Amid the crowd there was no face she could rest her eyes on except Anne's, but her childlike joy only isolated her further from Thérèse: her joy! As if she didn't know they would be separated this very night, and not just by space—but by what Thérèse was about to undergo—that irremediable thing to which her innocent body must submit. Anne remained safely on the shore where the intact creatures lived; Thérèse was going to join the troops of those who had served. She remembered how, in the sacristy, as she bent down to kiss the little laughing face lifted up to hers, she suddenly saw the nothingness out of which she had created a universe of vague sorrows and vague joys; she discovered, in the space of a few seconds, an infinite disproportion between the shadowy forces at work in her heart and Anne's pretty face, daubed with powder.

Long after that day, in Saint-Clair and in Bazas, people never talked about this Gamache-like[6] wedding (where more than a hundred tenant farmers and domestics had feasted and drunk beneath the oak trees) without recalling that the bride, "who wasn't what you'd call pretty but did have a certain charm," on that day seemed not just ugly but even hideous: "She didn't look like herself at all; it was like a different person . . ." People saw only how she looked different than she usually did; they blamed it on the white makeup, or on the heat; they had not recognized her true face.

On the evening of that half-peasant, half-bourgeois wedding day, groups of the guests crowded around their car, forcing it to slow down; the girls' dresses fluttered in the crowd. On the road strewn with acacia flowers, they drove past zigzagging carts driven by jokers who had drunk too much. Thérèse, thinking of the night that was coming, murmured, "It was horrible . . ." but then caught herself and said, "no—not so horrible." On their trip to the Italian lakes, had she suffered so much? No—she played the game; don't lie. A fiancé can be easily duped—but a husband! Lying with words is one thing, but lying with the body is quite a different art. To mime desire, joy, happy fatigue—not everybody can do that. Thérèse knew how to bend her body to these charades, and she took a bitter pleasure in the accomplishment. This unknown world of sensual pleasure into which the man forced her—her imagination helped her conceive that there was a real pleasure there for her too, a possible happiness—but what happiness? As when, before a country scene pouring with rain, we imagine to ourselves what it looks like in the sunshine—thus it was that Thérèse looked upon sensuality.

Bernard, the boy with the vacant stare, always uncomfortable when the sights didn't correspond exactly to his Baedeker,' and satisfied most when he had seen the greatest number of sights in the least possible time—what an easy dupe! He was as sunk in his pleasure as those sweet little pigs you can watch through the fence, snorting with happiness in their trough ("and I was the trough," thought Thérèse). He had the pigs' air of being busy, intent, serious; he was methodical. "Do you really think that's wise?" Thérèse risked asking, stupefied. He laughed; he reassured her. Where had he learned it, this ability to classify everything relating to the flesh, to distinguish the honorable caress from that of the sadist? Never a moment's hesitation. One night in Paris—where they had come on their return journey—Bernard made a show of walking out of a nightclub, shocked at the revue: "To think that foreign visitors will see that! What shame! And that's how they'll judge us . . ." Thérèse could only marvel that this so chaste man was the same one who would be making her submit, in less than an hour, to his patient inventions in the dark.

"Poor Bernard! He's no worse than others. But desire transforms the one who approaches us into a monster, a different being. Nothing separated us more than his delirium; I've often seen Bernard sink himself entirely in his pleasure—and me, I played dead, as if the slightest movement on my part could make this madman, this epileptic, strangle me. Most often, right at the point of his final bliss, he would suddenly discover his solitude; his dreary labor was interrupted. He would turn and find me there, as if I had been tossed up on a beach, teeth clenched, shivering with cold."

✦ ✦ ✦

Only one letter from Anne—the poor girl didn't like writing—but every line of it pleased Thérèse. A letter expresses not so much our real feelings as those that we have to feel so that it will be read with pleasure. Anne complained that she couldn't go Vilmeja since the arrival of the Azevedos' son; she had seen his lawn chair out among some ferns; tubercular people filled her with horror.

Thérèse often reread those pages, paying no attention to the others. So she was surprised (on the morning after the music hall incident), when the postman had come, to recognize Anne's handwriting on three envelopes. They had been sent on to Paris from various *postes restantes* because the couple had moved on so fast—"in a hurry," said Bernard, "to get back to our little nest," but in fact because they could no longer stand being alone together. He was dying of boredom, so far from his guns, his dogs, the café that made Picon grenadine with the taste that he so missed; and then there was this woman, so cold, so mocking, who took pleasure in nothing, who didn't like to talk about interesting things! As for Thérèse, she was anxious to get back to Saint-Clair in the same way that a deported criminal is who, bored with his provisional cell, is curious to see the island where he will have to spend the rest of his life. Thérèse carefully deciphered the date stamped on each of the three envelopes. And just as she opened the oldest one, Bernard let out an exclamation that she couldn't make out, for the window was open and the buses shifted gears noisily at their intersection. He had interrupted his shaving to read a letter from his mother. She saw again the sleeveless undershirt, the naked, muscular arms, the pale skin, and the sudden red flushing at his neck and face. On this July morning, the heat was already sulfurous and inescapable; the smoky sunshine only made the facades of the buildings beyond the balcony seem dingier. He had come up to Thérèse and cried out, "This is too much! Well! Your friend Anne, she's really going great guns! Who would ever have thought that my little sister . . ."

Thérèse shot him a questioning look.

"Could you believe it, she's gone and got herself infatuated with the Azevedo boy! Oh, it's perfect—the little tubercular case they refurbished Vilmeja for . . . But it sounds very serious. She says she's almost of age. Mother says she's completely mad. As long as the Deguilhems don't get wind of it! Young Deguilhem would be capable of breaking it off. You have some letters from her? Good, now we'll know—open them up!"

"I want to read them in order. And anyway, I don't want to show them to you."

He recognized this; it was typical Thérèse. She always had to complicate everything. But in any case, the essential thing was that she bring the girl back to her senses.

"My parents are counting on you: you can get her to do anything if, if . . . They're waiting for you, as for their savior."

While she dressed, he went off to send a telegram and get tickets on the Southern Express. She could begin packing the trunks.

"When are you going to read the letters? What are you waiting for?"

"For you to be gone."

✦ ✦ ✦

For a long time after he had gone, she remained on the bed, smoking cigarettes and gazing at the huge gold letters fixed to the balcony across the street; then she opened the first envelope. No, this couldn't be the same sweet little idiot; this couldn't be the little convent girl who had penned these burning words. This couldn't be that dried-up heart—because she did have a dried-up heart—and Thérèse, perhaps, knew it better than anyone. That heart could not have gushed itself out in this song of songs, this long delicious complaint of a woman possessed, of a flesh almost dead with ecstasy from the very first words:

When I first met him, I couldn't believe it was him: he was running along with his dog, calling out to him. How could I believe that this was the invalid—but he's not such an invalid; the family is only taking precautions because of what's happened. He's not even frail—more like thin—and then he's used to being coddled. You won't recognize me—I was the one who went to get his jacket when the heat let up . . .

If Bernard had come back into the room at that moment, he would have seen that the woman on the bed was not his wife but some unknown creature, foreign to him and nameless. She tossed away her cigarette and opened the second envelope:

I'll wait for as long as I have to; I'm not afraid of anything they can do, or any obstacles they put in my way; my love doesn't even feel it. They're taking me back to Saint-Clair, but that's close enough to Argelouse for me and Jean to meet. Do you remember the hunting cabin? It was you, dear Thérèse, who chose that place in advance, the place where I would come to know such happiness. Oh, but don't worry; we're not doing anything wrong. He's so delicate! You have no idea what a boy like this is like. He's studied and read a lot, like you, but I think that's okay for a boy, and I wouldn't dream of teasing him for it. What I wouldn't give to be as wise as you are! What is this happiness, dear Thérèse, that you already have and I don't yet, the very promise of which is such a thrill? When we were in the hunting cabin, where you always wanted us to bring our snacks, I stayed close to him and I sensed a happiness inside like something I could reach out and touch. I said to myself that there's still a joy even beyond this joy; and when Jean finally left, all pale, the memory of our caresses and the waiting for the next day to come left me deaf to all the complaints, the pleas, the insults of people who don't know this feeling . . . who have never known it. Oh Thérèse, pardon me: I'm talking about this happiness as if you didn't know it yourself, and after all I'm only a novice compared to you, and I'm absolutely sure you'll be on our side against all of them who are trying to hurt us . . .

Thérèse opened the third envelope—only a few scrawled words:

Come back, dear Thérèse: they've separated us; they're keeping me from seeing him. They think you'll be on their side. I told them I'd abide by your decision. I'll explain everything to you; he's not sick . . . I'm happy and I'm suffering. I'm happy to suffer for him and I love his sorrow as the sign of the love he feels for me . . .

Thérèse read no further. As she slipped the sheet back into the envelope, she saw a photograph that she had missed. Standing by the window, she contemplated his face. The boy's head seemed too big, because of his thick hair. She recognized the background: the hill where Jean Azevedo stood, like David (behind him, sheep were grazing). He had a jacket over his arm, and his shirt was partly open. Thérèse raised her eyes and was surprised at what she saw in the mirror. She had to make an effort to unclench her teeth, to swallow her saliva. She daubed some eau de cologne on her temples and forehead. "She knew this joy . . . and me then? Why not me?" The photograph lay on the table; near it, a hatpin glittered.

"I did that. I'm the one who did that . . ." In the jolting train which accelerated as it came to a descent, Thérèse repeated: "It was two years ago, in that hotel room, that I took the hatpin and pierced that boy's photograph where his heart was—not angrily, but calmly, as if it were a perfectly ordinary thing to be doing; I threw the pierced photo in the toilet; I flushed it."

✦ ✦ ✦

When Bernard came back in, he was pleased with her gravity, like that of a person who had reflected a great deal and had already drawn up a plan of action. But she shouldn't smoke so much; she was poisoning herself! Thérèse told him not to attach so much importance to the whims of a young girl. She would get everything straightened out. Bernard wanted Thérèse's reassurance, as he felt the joy of having their return tickets in his pocket, and felt flattered that his family had already sought out the help of his wife. He told her that, no matter what it cost, for the last supper of their trip, they would go to a restaurant in the Bois de Boulogne. In the taxi, he talked about his hunting plans; he was anxious to try out the dog that Balion had been training for him. His mother had written that the mare wasn't limping any more, thanks to the treatment . . . Hardly anyone was at the restaurant, where the sheer number of waiters intimidated them both. Thérèse recalled the odor: geraniums and brine. Bernard had never had Rhenish wine: "Back home, you can't get this." But then every day wasn't a festival day. Bernard's broad shoulders hid the room from Thérèse. Beyond the great windows, silent cars were stopping. She saw what she knew to be the temporal muscles moving by Bernard's ears. Immediately after his first gulps, he would start to become too red—this fine country boy who for three weeks now had missed the open space to burn off his food and alcohol. She did not hate him; but how strongly she wished she could be alone and think about her pain, and find the place where she hurt! If only he were not there; if only she didn't have to force herself to eat, to smile; if only she didn't have to compose her face to keep him from staring at her; if only she could let her spirit focus on this mysterious feeling of despair. Someone escapes from the desert island where you thought she would live with you till the end; she leaps over the abyss that separates you from the others, and rejoins them—or perhaps goes to another planet—but, no, who has ever been able to change planets? Anne had always belonged to the race of those who quite simply lived. The Anne she had seen on their solitary vacations, head on her knees, asleep—this was only a phantom. She had never known the real Anne de la Trave, the one who was meeting Jean Azevedo in an abandoned hut between Saint-Clair and Argelouse.

"What's wrong? Aren't you eating? We shouldn't leave any of this for them, considering what it costs; that'd be a shame. Is it the heat? You aren't going to faint, are you? This could be the sickness—already."

She smiled; or rather, her lips alone smiled. She said she was thinking about this business with Anne (she had to talk about Anne). Bernard declared he was perfectly confident about it all now that she had taken the matter into her hands. Thérèse asked him why her parents were so hostile to the match. He thought she was making fun of him, and begged her not to talk riddles to him:

"First, you know perfectly well that they're Jews. Mother knew the Azevedo grandfather, who refused to be baptized."

But Thérèse argued that the oldest and finest families in Bordeaux were Portuguese Jews:

"The Azevedos walked tall in the streets of the cities when our ancestors were groaning with fever in their marshlands."

"Look, Thérèse—don't argue for the sake of argument. All these Jews together are worth . . . and besides, it's a degenerate family, tubercular down to the bone, everybody knows it."

She lit a cigarette with a gesture that had always shocked Bernard.

"Remind me, how did your grandfather die, and your great-grandfather? You were anxious to know, marrying me, what disease took my mother off? Don't you think that we could find enough tuberculars and syphilitics among our ancestors to poison the whole universe?"

"You're going too far, Thérèse; permit me. Even in jest, and to get a rise out of me, don't ridicule the family."

He puffed out his chest, irritated—wanting both to take a high line and yet not to appear ridiculous to Thérèse. But she insisted:

"Our families make me laugh, with their prudence, like moles! This horror of what might be hereditary defects—it's only equaled by their indifference to the much more numerous ones they don't know about. You yourself, you use the expression 'secret diseases,' right? Well, the diseases that are most threatening to the whole race, aren't they by definition secret? Our families never think about these things, but for all that they're awfully good at keeping their dirt covered up. If it weren't for the domestics, we'd never know anything. Fortunately, there are the domestics . . ."

"I'm not going to respond to you. When you start in on these attacks, the best thing is just to let you finish. I'm only half angry with you; I know you're amusing yourself. But when we get home, remember, this won't do. We don't make jokes on the topic of the family."

The family! Thérèse let her cigarette go out. Her gaze fixed, she seemed to see that prison with its innumerable wardens at the ready, that cell covered with ears and eyes where she would wait for her death to come—immobile, bent down, chin on her knees, arms around her legs.

"Come on, Thérèse; don't look like that. If you could see how you look . . ."

She smiled and put the mask back on.

"I was kidding! How silly you are, sweetheart."

But in the taxi, when Bernard drew close to her, she pushed him away with her hand.

That last night before they returned home, they went to bed at nine. Thérèse took a pill, but she was too anxious for sleep to come, and it would not come. She had almost dozed off when Bernard, muttering something incomprehensible, rolled over; then she felt the big, hot body next to hers. She pushed him back and then, to escape from his heat, moved over to the edge of the bed, but after a few minutes he rolled toward her again, as if his sleeping flesh survived the absent spirit and was confusedly seeking its accustomed prey. Brutally, but still without awaking him, she shoved him away. Oh, to shove him once and for all—to hurl him off the bed, into the shadows!

Across nocturnal Paris, the cars' horns responded to each other like the dogs and roosters at Argelouse when the moon shines. No cool air ascended from the street. Thérèse lit the bed lamp and, her elbow on the pillow, looked at the motionless man next to her—this man in his twenty-seventh year. He had pushed back the covers; his breathing was inaudible; his tousled hair fell over his still-youthful forehead, his unwrinkled temples. He slept, Adam disarmed and naked, a deep, seemingly eternal sleep. The wife, throwing the covers over him, got out of bed seeking the letter whose reading he had interrupted, and brought it back by the lamp.

If he told me to follow him, I'd leave without even a glance backward. We stopped at the edge, the extreme edge of the ultimate caress, but through his own will power, not from my resisting. Or rather, it was he who resisted me, and I was the one who wanted to explore those extreme places where, he tells me, just getting close to them is the greatest of joys; he says we must always stop just this side of it. He's proud of always applying the brakes on the slopes; he says once you start down that way, everything else goes with you . . .

Thérèse opened the window, tore the letters into tiny pieces, bending over the stone abyss, while a solitary cart echoed down the street in the predawn hour. The paper fragments whirled, some landing on the balconies below. This odor of vegetation that she smelled—from what distant countryside had it blown here, into this concrete desert? She imagined the stain her body would make on the street, and the officials and the curious standing around it . . . Too vivid an imagination for suicide, Thérèse. In fact, though, she did not want to die; she felt the call of an urgent task, but not one of vengeance or hatred—but that little fool down there in Saint-Clair, who believed happiness was possible, she had to learn, as Thérèse had, that it doesn't exist. If they never had anything else in common, they would have that: the absence of any higher duty, the impossibility of everything except these low, everyday habits—solitude without any consolation. Dawn lit up the rooftops. She rejoined her husband on the bed, but as soon as she lay down, he rolled toward her.

She awoke, suddenly lucid and rational: why had she seen such a problem? The family had asked for her help, and she would do exactly what the family asked; thus she would stay precisely on course. Thérèse had agreed when Bernard said it would be a disaster if Anne didn't marry Deguilhem. The Deguilhems were not of their class; the grandfather had been a shepherd . . . Yes, but they did have the best pines in the region; and Anne after all is not so rich; she would get nothing from her father's side but some vineyards near Langon, and they were flooded one year out of every two. Anne must not fail to marry Deguilhem. The odor of hot chocolate in the room nauseated Thérèse; this light sickness confirmed all the other signs: pregnant, already. "It's best to have it all at once," said Bernard; "later, you won't have to think about it." And he gazed with respect on this woman who carried within her body the future sole master of innumerable pines.

V

Saint-Clair, soon! Saint-Clair . . . Thérèse now took the measure of the path down which her thoughts had been wandering. Would Bernard be willing to come down the path with her? She dared not hope that he would agree to walk, slow as she was, down such a twisting trail. And anyway, none of this had brought her to the essence yet: "When I've managed to bring him along to where I am now, I still won't have any of it figured out." She bent over the enigma of herself, examining the young bourgeois wife whose wisdom everyone praised around the Saint-Clair house, reliving the first weeks she had lived in her in-laws' cool, dark house. On one side of the living room the shutters were always closed, but on the left was a grille through which one could see the garden, bright with heliotrope, geraniums, petunias. Between the old couple, who posted themselves in the corner of the little, shadowy room, and Anne wandering in the garden, beyond which she was forbidden to go, Thérèse shuttled back and forth, the confidante, the accomplice. She said to the de la Traves: "Loosen the leash a little bit; offer her a trip, some travel before she makes any decision; I can guarantee she'll agree to that. And in the meantime, I'll go to work." Really? The de la Traves divined that she meant she would go to meet the young Azevedo: "You won't win with a direct attack, Mother." According to Madame de la Trave, nothing had happened yet, thank God. The postmistress, Mademoiselle Monod, was the only one they'd told; she had intercepted some of Anne's letters. "The

Monod girl is as close as a tomb. And she's on our side—she won't be chattering to anyone."

"Let's try to cause the least possible suffering," said Hector de la Trave; but he, who until recently had always given in to Anne's most absurd whims, now agreed with his wife, saying, "You can't make an omelet without breaking some eggs," and "She'll thank us some day." True, but in the meantime, wouldn't the girl become sick? The parents grew quiet and gazed off vaguely; no doubt they were picturing their daughter, who refused all food, consumed under the hot sun; she paced aimlessly, softly, crushing the flowers she didn't even see, a captive doe in search of some way out . . . Madame de la Trave shook her head: "I can't eat and drink for her, can I? She stuffs herself with fruit from the garden, so as to be able to leave her plate untouched at mealtime." And Hector: "She'd condemn us later on if we did give our consent. And it would be because of the sickly children she'd bring into the world . . ." His wife said he appeared to be looking for excuses: "Fortunately, the Deguilhems haven't returned yet. We're lucky that the idea of this marriage is the apple of their eye." They waited until Thérèse had left the room to ask each other: "But what sort of stuff did they put in her head at the convent? Thérèse says there's nothing worse, for turning a girl's head, than the love stories in the *Book of Good Stories*—but then she loves to be paradoxical.⁸ Anyway, Anne, thank God, was never infected with that mania for reading; I never had to warn her away from all that. In that respect, she's definitely one of the family. Do you think, if we could get her away for a while—do you remember how much good Salies did her after the bout of measles and bronchitis? We could go wherever she liked; I can't offer any more than that. Look, here's a girl with *so* much to complain about!" Hector sighed, "Oh, a trip with us—no never!" His wife, a little deaf, asked, "What did you say?" From the safe depths of this fortune he had married into, had the old man suddenly been struck with the memory of some clandestine lovers' trip, some blessed hours from his amorous youth?

♦ ♦ ♦

In the garden, Thérèse had rejoined the girl, whose dresses from last year had become too large for her. "Well?" cried Anne as her friend approached. Cinder pathways, dry, crunching prairie grass, the scent of burnt geraniums, and this girl even more consumed in the August afternoon than any of the plants—Thérèse could find nothing in her heart. Sometimes, threatening clouds would force them to shelter in the greenhouse; hailstones resounded on the windows.

"Why would it matter if you left here for a while, since you can't see him anyway?"

"I can't see him, but I know he's breathing ten kilometers from here. When the wind blows from the east, I know he can hear the bell at the same time I do. Would it be just the same to you if Bernard was in Paris instead of Argelouse? I can't see Jean, but I know he's nearby. On Sunday, at Mass, I try not to turn my head because from our pew only the altar is visible, and a pillar separates our pew from the rest of the congregation. But when we have to leave . . ."

"He wasn't there on Sunday?"

Thérèse knew it, knew that Anne, hurried along by her mother, had searched the crowd outside in vain for an absent face.

"Maybe he was sick. They intercept his letters; they won't let me know anything."

"Still, it's odd that he wouldn't have found some way of getting word to you."

"If you wanted to, Thérèse—but I know your position is delicate here."

"Agree to this trip, and while you're gone maybe . . ."

"I can't go away from him."

"But he'll go away in any case. In a few weeks, he'll be leaving Argelouse."

"Oh—be quiet! That's a horrible thought. And not a word from him to help me go on. I'm already dying of it: every minute, I have to remind myself of those words of his that gave me such joy. But I've repeated them so often that I'm no longer sure he really said them. Listen, the last time we met, I can hear him saying, 'There's nobody but you in my life . . .' He said that, or at least it was, 'There's nobody as dear as you in my life . . .' I can't remember exactly any more."

Her brows knitted, she sought for the consoling words, whose meaning she had already expanded to infinity.

"Well—what's he like, this boy?"

"You can't imagine."

"He's so different from all the others?"

"I'd like to describe him to you—but he's so far beyond anything I could express . . . But maybe you'd think he was perfectly ordinary. But I know he's not."

She couldn't provide any concrete details about the boy, she was so dazzled by her love. "For me," Thérèse thought, "passion would make me more, not less lucid. If I desired someone, not one detail would escape me."

"Thérèse, if I go on this trip, will you see him, and will you tell me exactly what he says? You'll give him my letters? If I go, if I have the courage to go . . ."

Thérèse left this kingdom of light and, like a grim wasp, penetrated again the dark living room where the parents waited for the heat to lessen, and for their daughter to wear down. It took many of these shuttlings back and forth to get Anne to decide to go on the trip. And Thérèse probably never would have succeeded if it hadn't been for the imminent return of the Deguilhems. Anne trembled before this new peril. Thérèse often said to her that for so rich a boy, "this Deguilhem isn't so bad."

"But Thérèse, I've scarcely looked at him: he wears glasses, he's bald, he's an old man."

"He's twenty-nine."

"As I said, he's an old man—and anyway, old or not . . ."

✦ ✦ ✦

At the evening meal, the parents talked about Biarritz, debating about a hotel. Thérèse observed Anne, motionless and spiritless. "Try a little—you have to try!" Madame de la Trave repeated. Anne raised the spoon to her mouth like an automaton. No light in her eyes. Nothing and nobody mattered for her except the one who was absent. Sometimes a smile played across her lips as she recalled a word she had heard, a caress she had received the time when, in the

cabin, the overstrong hand of Jean Azevedo had opened her blouse
a little. Thérèse watched Bernard bent over his plate: since he was
sitting against the light, she could not see his face, but she heard the
slow chewing, that rumination of the sacred food. She left the table.
Her mother-in-law said, "She doesn't like people to watch her eat.
I'd like to pamper her, but she doesn't like being fussed over. Her
bouts of sickness are the least anybody in her condition could have.
And it goes without saying, she smokes too much." And she
recalled her own memories of pregnancy: "I remember when I was
expecting, I had to breathe into a rubber ball; it was the only thing
that would settle my stomach."

♦ ♦ ♦

"Thérèse, where are you?"
"Here, on the bench."
"Oh yes—I can see your cigarette."
Anne sat down, leaning her head against Thérèse's stiffened
shoulder, and looking up at the stars, she said, "He sees these stars
too. He hears this Angelus . . ." And she said, "Kiss me, Thérèse."
But Thérèse didn't bend toward the confiding head. She only asked:
"Are you suffering?"
"No, tonight I'm not suffering; I've realized that, one way or
another, he and I will be together. I'm calm now. The main thing is
that he'll know, and that you'll tell him. I've decided to go on the
trip. But when I come back, no walls will be able to keep us apart;
sooner or later, I'll cast myself upon his heart; I'm as sure of that as
I am of my own life. No, Thérèse, don't be moral, not you at least;
don't talk about my family."
"I wasn't thinking of the family, dear Anne, but of him: you
can't just drop into a man's life like that. He has a family too, and
his own interests, his work, perhaps another relationship . . ."
"No, he told me, 'You're the only one in my life,' and another
time, 'Our love is the only thing that matters to me now . . ."
"'Now'?"
"What are you thinking? Do you think he only meant just at that
moment?"

Thérèse no longer needed to ask if she was suffering; she could hear the pain the darkness—but she heard it without any pity. Why would she have felt pity? How sweet it would be to repeat someone's name, a first name that designated a certain person to whose heart one was intimately tied! One's only thought being that he lived, that he breathed, that he slept that night, his head resting on his bent arm, that he'd awaken at dawn, that his young body's movements would displace the fog . . .

"Are you crying, Thérèse? You're crying for me? You do love me, don't you?"

The girl was on her knees, her head resting against Thérèse's side—and then suddenly she straightened herself:

"I felt something move against my forehead . . ."

"Yes, it's been moving now for a few days."

"The baby?"

"Yes; it's alive already."

They walked back to the house, intertwined as they had been on the Nizan road, on the Argelouse road. Thérèse recalled how she had been afraid for this quivering burden inside her, that her passions, the ones deepest within her, could penetrate that still unformed flesh. She could see herself again, that night, sitting in her room before the open window (Bernard had called out from the garden, "Leave the light off—mosquitoes"). She had counted the months left until the birth; she would have liked to know some God she could implore that this unknown creature, all intertwined with her insides already, would never show itself.

VI

It was strange, but Thérèse could only remember those days after the departure of Anne and her parents as a period of utter torpor. At Argelouse, where it was understood that she would find a way to work this Azevedo and get him to let go, she only thought about resting and sleeping. Bernard had agreed to stay not with her but at Thérèse's house, which was more comfortable, and where Aunt Clara's housekeeping spared him any difficulties. What did Thérèse care about what others thought? Let them take care of themselves. Nothing pleased her so much as this stupor; nothing mattered so much as staying in it until the child was born. Bernard irritated her every morning by reminding her of her promise to approach Jean Azevedo. But Thérèse rebuked him; she was beginning to find it harder to tolerate him. Maybe this mood is normal for someone in her condition, Bernard thought. He had started to feel the first signs of the obsession so common to men of his kind, though it is fairly rare before they turn thirty: the fear of death, surprising enough in a strong, well-built young man. But what could one reply to him when he protested, "You don't know how I feel"? The bodies of these big, idle, overfed men only appear to be powerful. A pine tree planted in a field and well fertilized will grow rapidly; but the heart of the tree rots and soon must be cut down, in the very moment of its greatest growth. "It's only nerves," people said to Bernard, but he felt the straw hidden beneath the surface of iron—the fatal crack deep inside. And then, the unimaginable happened: he stopped eating; he had no appetite. "Why don't you see a doctor?" He shrugged his shoulders, affecting detachment, but in fact the incertitude was less fearful than what might be the doctor's verdict of approaching death. One night, he startled Thérèse awake with a loud groan; Bernard took her hand and pressed it against his left side so she could count his heartbeats. She lit a candle, got up and mixed some valerian in a glass of water. It's only chance, she thought, that this mixture was a healing one—why shouldn't it be lethal? Nothing is really calm, nothing really sleeps if it's not for eternity. Why does this whining man feel such fear of what would calm him forever? He fell back asleep before she did. How could she wait for sleep next to this big body whose wheezings might turn into another bout of anguish? Thank God, he no longer approached her—making love seemed to him the worst possible exercise, potentially very bad for his heart. The roosters, at dawn, awakened the tenant farmers. The Saint-Clair Angelus bell tinkled in the east wind; finally Thérèse's eyes closed. Then the man's body started to move again: he dressed hurriedly, like a peasant, scarcely washing his face in the cold water. He rooted around in the kitchen like a dog, attracted to the leftovers in the pantry; he breakfasted, without bothering to use a plate, on what was left of a carcass, or on a slice of cold duck, or a bunch of grapes, or a crust rubbed with garlic— the only good meal he'd have all day. He tossed the crumbs to Flambeau and Diana; the dogs' jaws made smacking sounds. The fog had the scent of autumn. This was the hour when Bernard felt his best, sensing again his all-powerful youth. Soon some game birds flew past; he had to get busy on his decoys, to fool them. At eleven o'clock, he found Thérèse still in bed.

"So—what about Azevedo? You know that mother is expecting news at Biarritz, poste restante?"

"And your heart?"

"Don't mention my heart. As soon as you start talking about it, I start feeling it again. I suppose that proves that it's only nerves . . . Do you think it's nerves too?"

She never gave him the reply he wanted.

"You never know; you're the only one who knows what you're feeling. Your father dying from angina shouldn't matter—not at your age. It seems that the heart is the weak point for the Desqueyroux family. How funny you are, Bernard, with your fear of death!

Don't you have a sense, as I do, of how deeply useless we are? No? Don't you think that the lives of people like us already bear a strong resemblance to death?"

He shrugged his shoulders; her paradoxes made him sleepy. This sort of talk didn't require any cleverness; all you have to do is take whatever position is the opposite of the reasonable one. But she was wrong, he added, to expend all this on him: it would be better to save it for her interview with the Azevedo boy.

"You know he'll be leaving Vilmeja around the middle of October?"

◆ ◆ ◆

At Villandraut, the station just before Saint-Clair, Thérèse wondered, "How can I persuade Bernard that I was not in love with that boy? He's surely going to believe that I adored him. Like all those people who have never known what love is, he'll believe that the kind of crime I'm accused of could only spring from passion." Bernard would have to understand that, at that time, she was far from hating him—though his presence was often unwelcome; but she never imagined that any other man would have been any help to her. Bernard, when all was said and done, was not so bad. She detested the way novels sometimes depicted the kind of extraordinary people one would never meet in real life.

The only superior man she had ever known—that would have to be her father. She made an effort to see some grandeur in that stubborn, defiant radical who operated in various guises. He was a business owner (besides the sawmill at Bazas, he processed his own resin, and that of his relatives, at a factory in Saint-Clair). And he was above all a politician, whose curt manners worked against him, though he was always influential throughout the prefecture. And then his contempt for women—even for Thérèse in the days when everyone praised her intelligence. And now, after all this drama, his view was only confirmed: "They're all hysterics when they aren't idiots," he had repeated to the attorney. He was a nonbeliever and anticlerical, but always modest and chaste. Though he would sometimes hum one of Béranger's refrains,' he couldn't tolerate certain subjects being raised around him, reddening like a teenager. Bernard had heard from Monsieur de la Trave that Larroque had been a virgin when he married: "Since he became a widower, people have often told me they've never known him to have a mistress. Quite a character, your father!" Yes, he was a character. But though, away from him, she embellished her image of him, when he was nearby she could only see his vulgarity. He rarely came to Saint-Clair, a little more often to Argelouse, because he didn't like meeting the de la Traves. In their presence, forbidden to talk politics, the conversation after the soup course grew idiotic to him, and he started to get bitter. Thérèse would have been ashamed to join in the talk, taking pride in not opening her mouth, unless the conversation turned to religion. In that case, she rushed to support her father. Voices were raised, to the point where Aunt Clara herself picked up bits and pieces of the subject and threw herself into the battle, giving free rein to her old radical passions in the horrendous voice of a deaf woman: "Who knows what really goes on in those convents?" Though ultimately, Thérèse thought, Clara was more of a believer than any de la Trave, she was engaged in open war with the infinite Being who had allowed her to be both deaf and ugly, and to end her life without ever having been loved or possessed. After the day Madame de la Trave got up and stalked away from the table, everyone agreed to avoid metaphysics from then on. And politics was enough to get people enraged with each other—people who, whether on the left or the right, all abided by the one essential principle: property is the sole good in this world, and life is not worth living if one doesn't own land. But should there be limitations to ownership? And if so, to what extent? Thérèse, who had "property in her blood," would have enjoyed cynically calling the principle into question, for she hated the hypocrisy under which Larroque and the de la Traves masked their common passion. When her father proclaimed to her his "unfailing devotion to democracy," she interrupted him with, "Don't make such an effort; we're alone." She said that the sublime in politics nauseated her; the tragedy of class conflict escaped her altogether in that region where even the poorest owned some property and aspired to nothing more, where the universal love of land, hunting, eating, and drinking created a tight-knit fraternity of all, bourgeois and peasant alike. But Bernard was different; he had some education; people said that he had pulled himself up out of the rut. Thérèse even congratulated herself on his being a man with whom one could converse: "all in all, quite superior to his environment." That was how she saw him until the day she met Jean Azevedo.

◆ ◆ ◆

It was the season when the night's coolness lasted through the morning; and after lunchtime, hot as the sun was, a little fog announced from afar the coming of dusk. The first game birds flew past, and Bernard didn't return to the house until night. But that day, after a bad night, he had rushed off to Bordeaux to have himself examined by a doctor.

"I didn't desire anything in particular then," thought Thérèse. "I went out at one point down the road, because a pregnant woman is supposed to walk a bit. I avoided the woods with all the hunting blinds, where you have to stop constantly and whistle, then wait for the hunter to call out that you can proceed. But sometimes a long whistle responds to yours: a flight of birds is in sight among the oaks; you have to crouch down so as not to startle them. Then I went back to the house; I dozed awhile before the kitchen fireplace, Aunt Clara taking care of anything I needed. Like a god who pays no attention to his servant—so I was with that old woman, snuffling out her stories about kitchens and farms. She talked and talked, just to avoid having to listen, almost always telling lurid anecdotes about the farmers she looked after with her clear-sighted, unsentimental devotion: old men reduced to dying of hunger, condemned to work up until the moment of death, abandoned invalids, women enslaved to exhausting labor. With an air of cheerfulness, Aunt Clara told their most atrocious stories in an innocent patois. In truth though, she only loved me, the only one who never even noticed her down on her knees, unlacing my shoes, removing my stockings, warming my feet in her aged hands.

"'Balion will be coming for his instructions for tomorrow when he goes to Saint-Clair.' Aunt Clara went through the list she prepared for him, adding in prescriptions for the sick in Argelouse.

'First, go to the pharmacy; Darquey won't need much time to mix up the medicine . . .'

"My first meeting with Jean . . . I must remember every detail. I had decided to go to that hunting cabin where Anne and I had gone and where I knew she liked to meet him. No, this was not some kind of pilgrimage for me. But the pine trees on this side had grown too thick for watching for birds there; there was no danger of disturbing hunters. The cabin was no longer any good for hunting because the forest surrounding it hid the horizon. The treetops no longer allowed for those wide avenues of sky where the observer can see the flights coming or going. Remember: that October, it was still burning hot; I struggled along on the sandy path, harassed by flies. My stomach was so heavy! I looked forward to sitting down on the rotting bench in the cabin. Just as I opened the door, a young man was coming out, not wearing a hat. I recognized Jean Azevedo at once, and at first I thought I had interrupted some rendezvous, because he seemed so flustered. But I stepped aside in vain; it was strange that he immediately asked me to stay. 'Please come in Madame; I assure you you're not bothering me at all.'

"Since he insisted, I went in the cabin, but I was surprised to see nobody else there. Perhaps the shepherdess had fled through some other exit? But I heard no twig cracking. He had recognized me too, and quickly Anne's name came to his lips. I was seated, and he standing, as in his photograph. I gazed at the spot, through his silk shirt, where I had plunged the hatpin—gazed with a detached curiosity. Was he handsome? A strong forehead, the soft eyes of his race, cheeks that were too full—and then, what has always disgusted me most in boys that age: pimples, the signs of blood in motion, everything running, and above all those moist palms that he rubbed with a handkerchief before shaking your hand. But he had a burning gaze; I liked his large mouth, always a little open, revealing keen teeth—like the mouth of an overheated young dog. And me, what was I like? All family, I recall. I took the high line at once, accusing him solemnly of 'bringing trouble and division into an honorable family.' Oh! Remember his unfeigned astonishment, his childlike burst of laughter: 'What, do you think I want to marry her? Do you think I'm soliciting that honor?' I tried to measure at once this abyss yawning between the passion of Anne and the indif-

ference of the boy. He defended himself heatedly: of course, who
wouldn't give in to the charm of so delicious a girl? He admitted
playing with her, but precisely because there could be no question
of marriage between them, the play seemed harmless. Yes, he
admitted pretending to feel as Anne did—and when I, perched on
my high horse, interrupted him, he replied vehemently that Anne
herself would witness for him that he knew never to go too far. And
as for the rest, no doubt Mademoiselle de la Trave owed to him the
only hours of real passion that she would ever know in her dreary
existence. 'You tell me she's suffering, Madame, but do you honestly believe she has anything better than this suffering to look forward to? I know you by reputation; I know that one can say things
to you and that you're not like the other people here. Before she sets
off on the gloomy journey of her life in that Saint-Clair house, I
provided her with some capital, a fund of sensations, of dreams—
which may save her from despair, or, in any case, from becoming a
brute.' I can't remember if I was frozen by this excess of preten-
sion, of affectation, or even if I was aware of it. In fact, his delivery
of all this was so rapid that at first I didn't follow; but I soon got
used to his volubility. 'To think me capable of desiring such a marriage, to throw my anchor down in that sand—or to run off to Paris
with a young girl? I still think of Anne as adorable, of course, and
in fact at the very moment you surprised me, I was thinking of
her . . . But how can a person settle down, Madame? Every minute
brings its own unique joy—a joy different from all those that have
come before it.'

"That young, animal eagerness and that intelligence, combined
in one person, seemed so strange to me that I listened without inter-
rupting. Yes, I definitely was dazzled: great God, here was something fresh! But I was. I can recall the sound of tramping feet and
the rough cries of shepherds signaling the approach of a flock. I
said to the boy that it might seem a bit comic if we were discovered
together in the cabin; I wanted him to reply that it would be better
to make no sound until the flock passed; I was thrilling to this
silence, this being close together, this complicity (and I was already
becoming demanding too, wanting each minute to bring me something to live for). But Jean Azevedo, without any protest, opened
the door and, ceremoniously, stepped aside. He only followed me to

Argelouse after being assured that I saw no problem in his doing so. That walk back seemed so rapid to me, but my companion found the time to touch on a thousand topics. Every subject I thought I knew something about, he somehow made it new again. For example, on the religious question, when I repeated what I was accustomed to saying to the family, he interrupted me: 'Yes, no doubt— but it's more complicated than that . . .' He managed, in fact, to cast some admirable light on the debate . . . But was it all that admirable, really? Today, I think I'd vomit if I tried to swallow some of that stuff: he said that he had long ago decided that nothing mattered but the search for, the pursuit of, God: 'To set off, take to the sea, flee like death those who think they've found Him, the ones who settle down, building their little shelters to sleep in; I've despised them for a long time . . .'

"He asked me if I'd read René Bazin's *Life of Father Foucauld*,[10] and when I affected to laugh, he assured me that the book had astonished him: 'To live dangerously, in the profoundest sense, maybe isn't so much to seek God but to find Him, and then to remain within His orbit.' He described 'the great adventure of the mystics,' and complained that his own temperament prevented him from trying it, 'but as far back as I can remember, I can't recall ever being pure.' So much immodesty, and that ease in opening himself up, made such a change for me from provincial discretion, from that silence in which, at our house, everyone buried his inner life! Even the gossips of Saint-Clair only touched on appearances; hearts were never uncovered. What do I know of Bernard, ultimately? Inside, he must be infinitely more than the caricature I content myself with, when I have to think about him. Jean talked on, and I remained mute. Nothing rose to my lips beyond the habitual phrases from our family conversations. Just as, around here, all the carts are 'on track,' which means just large enough so the wheels fit precisely within the ruts in the road—so until that day all my thoughts were 'on track' with my father's and my in-laws'. Jean Azevedo walked along, not wearing a cap; I can still see that shirt opened on his child's chest, his too-thick neck. Had I given in to physical charm? Oh God, no! But he was the first man I'd met for whom the inner life counted more than anything else. His teachers, his Parisian friends whose ideas he hurled at me constantly, along with the names of books that would change my thinking about this or that: he belonged, he said, to a numerous elite, to 'those who live.' He cited names, not even imagining that I might not have heard of them; and I pretended not to be hearing them for the first time.

"When the road turned and the Argelouse rye field appeared, I cried 'Already!' The scent of burnt grass hovered over this impoverished, cut-down earth that had yielded its rye. In a notch on the hill, a flock of sheep streamed like dirty milk, seeming to graze on the sand. Jean had to cross the field to get to Vilmeja. I said to him, 'I'll come with you; all these questions fascinate me.' But we found nothing more to say. The mown stems of rye cut through my sandals. I had the feeling that he wanted to be alone to pursue some line of thought that had occurred to him. I mentioned that we hadn't spoken of Anne; he countered that we weren't free to choose the subjects of our conversations or our meditations. He added grandly, 'We must adhere to the methods invented by the mystics . . . Beings like us always follow the current wherever it goes, obeying the turnings of the stream . . .' So he always brought everything back to his current reading. We arranged to meet and work out a plan of action regarding Anne. He spoke distractedly, and, without listening to a question I had asked, bent down: with a childlike gesture, he picked up a vine shoot, and put it first to his nose, then to his lips, and then held it out to me."

VII

Bernard, in the doorway, was watching out for Thérèse's return. "There's nothing wrong with me! There's nothing wrong," he cried out the minute he saw her dress in the dusk. "Can you believe it, built like I am, I'm anemic! Unbelievable, but true; you just can't judge by appearances. I have to start a treatment, the Fowler treatment; it's arsenic." The key is for me to get my appetite back."

Thérèse recalled that at first she had not been annoyed: everything that came toward her from Bernard irritated her less than usual (as if she were feeling only glancing blows). She didn't listen to him, her body and soul oriented now toward another universe where people were avid to know, to understand—and, in the phrase Jean had used with great self-satisfaction, "become what they truly were." When, at the table, she finally mentioned that she had met him, Bernard blurted out, "What? You didn't tell me? What a funny type you are! Well? What did you two decide?"

She improvised the plan that they would need to carry out: Jean Azevedo agreed to write Anne a letter in which he would gently remove all her hopes. Bernard guffawed when Thérèse explained that the young man wasn't at all interested in marriage: an Azevedo would not want to marry an Anne de la Trave! "Oh, are you crazy? It's simple: he knows it won't happen. Those people never take a risk when they're sure to lose. You're still pretty naïve, sweetheart."

Because of the mosquitoes, Bernard didn't want the lamp turned on, so he didn't see the way Thérèse looked at him. "He had

ered his appetite," as he put it. Already the Bordeaux doctor
ranted him life.

Did I see Jean Azevedo often after that? He left Argelouse
toward the end of October... We took perhaps five or six walks
together; I can only isolate the one where we were occupied in
drafting the letter to Anne. Naïve as he was, he would come up with
formulas he thought would be soothing, but which I knew, without
saying so to him, would devastate Anne. But our last walks are confused into one single memory. Jean Azevedo described Paris and
his friends to me, and I imagined a kingdom where the law was,
'Become yourself.' 'Here, you're condemned to lies until you die.'
Did he say this intentionally? What did he suspect about me?
According to him, I would find it impossible to go on enduring this
stifling climate. 'Look,' he said to me, 'at this immense and uni-
form surface of ice in which all these souls are frozen. Sometimes a
crevice opens, revealing black water below; someone falls and dis-
appears; the crust re-forms over him ... Because everyone, here as
elsewhere, is born with his own law; here as elsewhere, every destiny is unique, but for all that one must submit to the dismal destiny
of everyone else. A few resist—and hence those moments of drama
about which families keep silent. As they say here, "You mustn't
talk about it."'

"'Oh, yes!' I cried. 'Sometimes I've been curious about some
great-uncle, or some woman relative whose photos have disappeared from all the albums, and I've never, not once, received a
reply other than "He disappeared ... He had to disappear."'

"Did Jean Azevedo fear that sort of fate for me? He assured me
that he had never dreamed of saying such things to Anne because,
despite all her passion, she was an utterly simple soul, a little rest-
less now, but one who would soon enough willingly take on the
yoke. 'But you! I can sense a hunger and thirst for sincerity in your
words ...' Must I report all this exactly to Bernard? It's insane to
hope he'll understand any of it! But he must know, in any case, that
I didn't succumb without a fight. I remember telling the boy that his
smooth phrases were only a mask, a rationalization for assenting to
the vilest sort of depravity. I even had recourse to my memories of
the moral readings we'd been assigned in school. 'To be one's own
self?' I said. 'But we can only do that to the extent that we create

ourselves.' (No need to develop that now, but it might be ne
to develop it for Bernard.) Azevedo insisted that there was r
degeneration than that of destroying one's self. He clain.... ....
every hero and saint had to make the grand tour of his self to discover his limits, and he repeated that 'we have to go beyond the self
to find God.' And again: 'Accepting the self requires that the best
among us confront the self, openly and in free combat without sub-
terfuge, and that's why it often happens that the most liberated ones
convert to the strictest religion.'

"Don't discuss the foundations of this moral philosophy with
Bernard—and even grant him that there is an impoverished soph-
istry in it. But he must understand, he must be made to understand
just how a woman like me can be touched, and what I felt that
evening in the dining room in Argelouse. Bernard, in the kitchen
adjoining, was taking off his boots and recounting in patois the
day's hunting. The woodcocks fought, ruffling the bag he placed on
the table. Bernard ate slowly, delighted with his regained appetite,
and counted out his Fowler drops lovingly. 'This is health,' he
repeated. A large fire was burning and, at dessert, he had only to
turn his chair to bring his feet, in their felt slippers, up to the grate.
His eyes closed over the *Petit Gironde* newspaper. Sometimes he
snored, but also I could often hear no breathing at all. Balionte's[12]
slippers shuffled across the kitchen; soon she brought out the can-
dles. And then there was silence—the silence of Argelouse! People
who don't know this forsaken region don't know what silence is. It
surrounds the house like a solid thing born out of the thick mass of
forest where nothing lives, only the occasional hooting owl—at
night, we think we can hear the sobs we stifle.

"It was chiefly after Azevedo's departure that I came to know it,
this silence. When I knew that I'd see him the next day, his presence tamed the external shadows; knowing he was asleep nearby
populated the empty lands and the night for me. But once he was
gone from Argelouse, after our last meeting when he said we would
meet again a year later, saying it full of hope that by then, he said, I
would have figured out how to free myself . . . And today I don't
know really whether he was just saying it lightly or whether he had
some other motive; I'm inclined to think that Parisian couldn't take
the silence any more, and that he only really liked me because I was

his only auditor . . . But once he'd left me I felt like I'd entered into an endless tunnel, sinking into a shadow that grew and grew, and sometimes I wondered if I would reach the open air before I suffocated. Until the birth, in January, nothing else happened . . ."

◆ ◆ ◆

Here, Thérèse hesitated, and forced herself to remember what happened in the Argelouse house the day after Jean's departure. "No, no," she thought, "all that has nothing to do with what I must explain to Bernard tonight; I can't let myself get lost on those paths that don't lead anywhere." But thoughts are rebellious; they can't be stopped from running where they will. Thérèse could not erase that October night from her memory. On the floor above, Bernard was undressing; Thérèse waited for the fire to burn out before joining him, happy to be alone for a little while—what was Jean Azevedo doing at this moment? Perhaps he was drinking in the little bar he had mentioned; perhaps (it was a fine night) he was in a car with a friend, driving through the deserted Bois de Boulogne. Perhaps he was working at his desk while Paris rumbled on in the distance; he was the one who created his own silence, overcoming the noisy hubbub of the world—his silence wasn't imposed on him from outside, like the silence suffocating Thérèse; his silence was his own work, extending no farther than the light of his lamp, its rays falling on his books . . . Thus Thérèse dreamed; and suddenly the dog was barking, then whining, and a voice it recognized was soothing it. Anne de la Trave opened the door. She had come on foot, at night, all the way from Saint-Clair, her shoes thick with mud. She looked as if she had aged. She threw her hat on the armchair and asked, "Where is he?"

Thérèse and Jean, their letter finished and posted, had thought the affair was over. They never dreamed that Anne would hang on—as if she would submit to rational argument, when this was a matter of life itself for her! She had managed to escape her mother's surveillance and got herself on a train. On the dark Argelouse road, she was guided by the light stream of sky between the treetops. "Everything depended on seeing him; if she saw him, he would relent; she had to see him." She stumbled, twisting her feet in the road's ruts, in her urgent need to get to Argelouse. And now Thérèse told her that Jean was gone, that he was in Paris. Anne shook her head, saying no, she didn't believe it. She needed not to believe it, to keep from collapsing in fatigue and despair.

"You're lying; you've always lied."

When Thérèse protested, she added, "Oh, you've done a fine job, the family representative! You pretend to be liberated . . . But since your marriage you've become a true woman of the family. Oh, yes, I understand; you were doing a good thing, betraying me in order to save me, isn't that it? And I'm so very grateful for your efforts!"

She reopened the door, and Thérèse asked where she was going.

"To Vilmeja, to his place."

"I'm telling you he's been gone for two days."

"I don't believe you."

She went out. Thérèse lit the vestibule's hanging lantern and caught up with her.

"You're lost, Anne: You're on the path to Biourge. Vilmeja is that way."

They walked through the fog rising above the fields. Dogs awakened. And here were the oak trees of Vilmeja, the house not sleeping but dead. Anne rounded the empty sepulchre, banging on the doors with both fists. Thérèse stood motionless in the grass with her lantern. She saw her friend like a thin ghost, peering into every window on the ground floor. Anne was repeating his name, but quietly, knowing how useless it was. Sometimes she would be hidden by the house, and then reappear; returning to the front door, she slipped down on the threshold, knotting her arms around her knees. Thérèse helped her up and led her off. Anne stumbled, repeating, "I'll go to Paris tomorrow. Paris is not that big; I'll find him in Paris . . ." But she said this in the tone of a child who has reached the limits of her resistance and is already beginning to surrender.

✦ ✦ ✦

who had been awakened by their voices, now awaited
iving room in his robe. Thérèse was wrong to seek the
vhat then passed between the brother and sister. "This
of roughly taking a desperate girl by the wrists, pulling her up to a room on the upper floor and locking the door, this is
your husband, Thérèse, this Bernard who in two hours will be your
judge. The spirit of the family inspires him in everything he does,
saves him from every possible hesitation. He knows, in every situation, what will be in the family's best interests. You, with all your
anguish, you're preparing your lengthy defense; but it's only men
without Bernard's sort of principles who are capable of giving in to
another's arguments. Bernard will mock you: 'I know what I have
to do.' He always knows what to do. If ever he does hesitate, he
soon says, 'We've talked it over among the family, and we've
decided that . . .' How can you doubt for a minute that he hasn't
already made his judgment? Your fate is fixed already, and fixed
forever; you'd do just as well now just to sleep."

VIII

After the de la Traves brought the vanquished Anne back to Saint-Clair, Thérèse never left Argelouse up until the time she gave birth. She had become only too familiar with the silence during those endless November nights. A letter mailed to Jean Azevedo went without a reply. Probably he felt this provincial woman wasn't worth the tedium of a correspondence. And besides, a pregnant woman doesn't make for a beautiful memory. Perhaps at the distance he now was, he thought of Thérèse as boring, an imbecile, restrained by artificial complications and attitudes. But how much of her could he have understood, with her deceptive simplicity, her direct gaze, her confident gestures? In fact, he thought of her, like Anne, as someone who could be taken at her word, someone who could leave it all behind and follow him. Jean Azevedo detested those women who surrender too soon, before their assailant can give up the siege. He feared nothing so much as victory, and the fruits of victory. Thérèse, however, made an effort to live in the boy's universe; but the books Jean admired, which she ordered from Bordeaux, were incomprehensible to her. There was never anything to do! She couldn't be expected to help with preparing the baby clothes. "That's not her job," Madame de la Trave liked to say. Many women died in childbirth out in the country. Thérèse made Aunt Clara cry by insisting that she would end up as her mother had, that she was sure she wouldn't recover. She didn't miss the chance to add, "Dying was all the same to her." A lie! She had never so ardently wanted to live—and Bernard had never shown so much solicitude. "He's not so worried about me as about what I'm carrying inside me. He yammers at me, in that hideous accent, 'Take some more of the purée . . . Don't eat fish . . . You've walked enough for today . . .' I was no more touched by all that than a wet nurse is, being groomed for the sake of the quality of her milk. The de la Traves venerated me as a sort of sacred vessel, the receptacle of their progeniture; there's not a doubt that, if things had turned out that way, they would have sacrificed me for that embryo. I was losing all sense of my individual existence. I was only the vine; in the eyes of the family, all that counted was the fruit of my womb."

◆ ◆ ◆

"Till the end of December, I had to live in those shadows. As if the innumerable pines weren't enough, the rain was uninterrupted, pouring down around the dark house like a million moving prison bars. When the only road to Saint-Clair looked as if it would become impassable, they brought me to town, to the house scarcely less dark than Argelouse. The old plane trees outside still fought for their last leaves with the rainy wind. Aunt Clara, unable to live anywhere but Argelouse, didn't want to set up house at my bedside, so instead she frequently made the trip in 'on-track' cabriolet, in all kinds of weather. She brought me the little tidbits I'd loved as a girl, and that she thought I still loved—those gray balls of rye and honey called *miques*, and the cake they call *fougasse* or *roudmajade*. I never saw Anne except at meals, and she no longer spoke to me. Resigned, or rather worn down, she seemed to have lost all her youthfulness at one blow. Her hair, tied back too severely, revealed her unlovely, pale ears. No one ever spoke about Jean Deguilhem, but Madame de la Trave insisted that, if Anne hadn't said yes yet, she also hadn't said no. Oh, Jean had her figured out perfectly: it hadn't taken so very long for her to put on the bridle and begin to trot. Bernard was doing less well, since he'd gone back to drinking aperitifs. What did those people around me talk about? There was a lot about the priest, I recall (we lived across from the rectory). They busied themselves with discussing, for example, 'why he had crossed the square four times today, and each time he came back a different way . . ."

Based on some things Jean Azevedo had said, Thérèse began to pay more attention to this still-young priest who didn't communicate much with his parishioners. They thought he was arrogant: "He's not the type we want around here." During his rare visits to the de la Traves, Thérèse observed his whitening temples, his high forehead. No friends. How did he spend his evenings? Why had he chosen this life? "He's very precise," said Madame de la Trave; "he makes his devotions every night. But he lacks unction; he isn't what I'd call pious. And he drops everything for charity work." She lamented his breaking up the youth club's brass band; parents complained that he no longer went out on the soccer field with the children. "It's all very nice to keep your nose buried in books, but a parish can be quickly lost." Thérèse began to frequent the church to listen to him. "You've started doing this, little one, at just the time when your condition would excuse you from it." The priest's sermons on dogma and morality were impersonal. But Thérèse was intrigued by an inflection of his voice, a gesture he made; the words themselves sometimes seemed clumsier . . . Oh, maybe he could have helped untangle the confused world within her; he was different from the others, and he too had to play a tragic role: his cassock created a kind of desert around the man who wore it, and he had added this to his interior solitude. What comfort could he find in his daily rites? Thérèse would have liked to assist at the altar during weekday Mass when, with no other witness than the choirboy, he murmured some words while bent over a morsel of bread. But making such an approach would have seemed strange to the family and to the townspeople; everyone would have begun exclaiming that she had been converted.

As much as Thérèse suffered during that time, it was only the day after giving birth that she really ceased being able to tolerate living. Nothing showed on the outside; there were no scenes between her and Bernard, and she was more deferential to her in-laws than even Bernard was. And that was the tragedy, that there was no reason for the break. The outcome had been impossible to foresee; there had been no one moment when one could have changed things and prevented them from taking their lethal course.

To say that there had been some disagreement or misunderstanding implies that there had been some ground on which the principals met and collided, but Thérèse almost never engaged with Bernard and still less with her in-laws; it never occurred to her that she should respond to them. Did they even have a vocabulary in common? They gave different senses to basic words. If Thérèse had let a heartfelt scream escape from her, the family would have remarked only that the young woman loved her little whims. "When she gets started, I pretend not to listen," said Madame de la Trave, "and if she insists, I don't attach any importance to it; she knows that sort of thing won't work with us."

However, Madame de la Trave did not like one particular affectation of Thérèse's, her claiming she couldn't endure people saying how much little Marie resembled her mother. Those customary exclamations ("See that, now; you can't deny that . . .") threw the young woman into feelings she couldn't always dissemble. "This child looks nothing like me," she insisted. "Look at her dark complexion, her black eyes, and then look at my old photos: I was a fair child."

She didn't want Marie to resemble her. She wanted to have nothing in common with this flesh detached from hers. People started saying she lacked maternal feeling. But Madame de la Trave assured them that she loved her daughter in her own way. "True, you can't ask her to oversee a bath or change diapers; that's not in her line. But I've seen her sitting by the cradle for whole evenings, holding off on her smoking, just to watch the little one sleep. And anyway, we have a very good nurse, and then Anne is here too—oh, that one is going to make a terrific young mama!" It was true that Anne had come back to life as soon as there was a baby in the house. A cradle always attracts women, but Anne, more than the others, handled the infant with a profound joy. To get fully free access to the baby, she had made peace with Thérèse, though nothing remained of their old tenderness except a few gestures and familiar phrases. Anne feared above all else that Thérèse would develop a maternal jealousy: "The little one knows me better than her mother. As soon as she sees me, she smiles. The other day, I had her in my arms, and when Thérèse tried to take her, she started howling. She prefers me—to the point where it's a little uncomfortable . . ."

♦ ♦ ♦

Anne was wrong to feel uncomfortable. At that moment in her life, Thérèse felt as detached from her child as from everyone else. She saw other people and things, even her own body and mind, as a kind of mirage, a vapor suspended outside of her. In this nothingness, only Bernard took on a hideous reality: his corpulence, his nasal voice, and that peremptory tone, that self-satisfaction. To get out of this world—but how? And where to go? The first warm days depressed Thérèse. There was no warning of what she was about to do. What happened that year? She could recall no incident, no quarrel. She remembered loathing her husband more than usual on Corpus Christi day, when she watched the procession through the half-closed shutters. Bernard was almost the only one walking behind the canopy. The village had become deserted in just a few minutes, as if it had been a lion, not a lamb, that had been released into the streets . . . Some people had holed up, to avoid having to remove their hats or to kneel. Once the peril had passed, doors opened up, one by one. Thérèse had stared at the priest, who advanced with his eyes almost closed, holding that strange object in both hands. His lips were moving: who was he talking to, with that sorrowful air about him? And soon, behind him, came Bernard, who was "performing his duty."

♦ ♦ ♦

Week after week passed without a drop of rain falling. Bernard lived in terror of a fire starting, and he once again began to feel his "heart problem." Five hundred hectares had burned outside Louchats. "If the wind had shifted to the north, my Balisac pines would have gone up." Thérèse expected something to come from that unalterable sky. It would never rain again. One day, the whole forest would crackle around them, and the town itself would not be spared. Why weren't the region's towns burning already? She found it unjust that the flames always chose the trees and not the people. The family had endless discussions about sinister causes: a tossed-away cigarette? Deliberate arson? Thérèse fantasized that one night she would get up, leave the house, go out to the thickest part of the forest, and toss aside her cigarette and watch an immense smoke tarnish the dawn sky . . . But she chased the thought away, having the love of pines in her blood; it was not toward trees that her hatred was directed.

+ + +

And now was the moment to look squarely at what she had done. What explanation could she give Bernard? Nothing for it but to bring him step by step to how the thing came to pass. It was the day of the great fire near Mano. Some men came into the dining room where the family was at the table, eating hurriedly. Some insisted that the fire was very distant from Saint-Clair, while others argued for sounding the alarm bells immediately. The perfume of burnt resin impregnated the day; the sun appeared soiled. And now Thérèse could again envision Bernard, his head turned to listen to Balion's report, while his large, hairy hand hovered, momentarily forgotten, above the glass, while the Fowler drops fell into the water. Thérèse thought of warning him that he had doubled his usual dose, while he went on to drink it all off at one gulp. Everyone had left the table—except for Thérèse, who sat on, cracking open fresh almonds, uninterested in all the drama going on around her, as she was uninterested in any drama other than her own. The alarm bell did not sound. Finally Bernard returned: "For once, you were right not to be concerned—the fire's on the other side of Mano." He asked, "Did I take my drops?"—and without waiting for her reply, he put another dose in his glass. She kept silent out of laziness, probably, and out of fatigue. What was she hoping for at that moment? "It's impossible that I actually planned to keep silent."

However, that night, while Bernard in his bed vomited and wept, Doctor Pedemay asked her about the events of the day, and she said nothing about what she had seen at the table. It would have been easy to direct the doctor's attention to the arsenic without compromising herself. She could have found a phrase like, "I can't remember exactly, we were all so agitated over the fire, but now it does seem to me that he took a double dose . . ." But she remained mute; had she even been tempted to speak up? The act had, during dinner, been within her without her knowing it, and now it began to emerge from the depths of her being—unformed still, but swimming up closer to her awareness.

After the doctor left, she watched Bernard, finally asleep, and thought, "Nothing can prove that it was *that*; it could have been an attack of appendicitis, though there were no other symptoms . . . or a case of stomach flu." But two days later Bernard was back on his feet. "He was lucky if it was *that*." Thérèse could not have sworn to it; she wanted to be sure. "Yes—I didn't feel at all that I was in the grip of some horrible temptation; it was more a matter of a curiosity that was a bit dangerous to satisfy. The first day when, before Bernard came in the room, I put some Fowler drops in the water, I remember repeating to myself: 'Just this once, just to be absolutely sure . . . I'll find out whether this is what made him sick. Just once, and it will be over.'"

✦ ✦ ✦

The train slowed, gave a long sigh, and then started up again. Two or three lights in the darkness: the Saint-Clair station. But Thérèse was not looking at it, for she was engulfed in the abyss of her crime; it had breathed her in. And what followed, Bernard knew as well as she did: the sudden return of the sickness, and Thérèse watching over him night and day, though she was exhausted and found herself at one point unable to swallow a thing—at which point Bernard suggested she try the Fowler treatment, and she got a prescription from Doctor Pedemay. The poor doctor! He was shocked at the greenish liquid Bernard was vomiting, and he had never believed there could be such a discrepancy between a patient's pulse and his temperature; he had often enough seen typhus cases where a calm pulse combined with a high fever—but what could explain this pounding pulse and this below-normal temperature? An influenza, no doubt; influenza—the word explained everything.

Madame de la Trave thought of calling in a well-known medical consultant, but she didn't want to hurt the pride of her old friend the doctor; and then Thérèse feared it would frighten Bernard. But toward mid-August, after a particularly alarming episode, Pedemay himself sought the advice of one of his colleagues; fortunately, Bernard improved the next day, and a few weeks later people began speaking more hopefully of a convalescent period. "I've gotten out of this one pretty well," said Doctor Pedemay. "If the great man had had the time to come, he'd have taken credit for the cure."

Bernard moved back to Argelouse, believing himself sufficiently cured to get back to his hunting. During this period, Thérèse was frequently exhausted: Aunt Clara had a rheumatic attack, so everything fell to Thérèse—two invalids and a baby, along with all the chores Aunt Clara normally did. Thérèse willingly took over Clara's work with the Argelouse poor. She made the rounds of tenant farms, busying herself as her aunt did with getting prescriptions filled, paying for them out of her own purse. Passing close by the Vilmeja farms did not sadden her; she never thought of Jean Azevedo, nor of anyone else at all. She was alone, moving through the darkest part of a dark tunnel, in a kind of vertigo. Like an animal, she did not reflect on her situation but only felt the urgent need to get out of this darkness, to reach open air—and quickly!

At the beginning of December, Bernard's illness returned; he woke up one morning shivering, his limbs inert and numb. And then, what followed! Monsieur de la Trave had brought in a consulting physician from Bordeaux; after examining the sick man, he remained silent for a long time. (Thérèse held the lamp, and Balionte remembered later that she was whiter than Bernard's sheets.) On the ill-lit landing, Pedemay lowered his voice, knowing Thérèse was listening, and explained to his colleague that Darquey, the pharmacist, had shown him two forged prescriptions. On the first, the forger had written "Fowler drops"; the other called for strong doses of chloroform, digitalis, and aconite. Balion had brought them to the pharmacy along with many others. Darquey, feeling tormented at having dispensed the toxins, had run to Pedemay the next morning . . . Yes, Bernard knew all these things as well as Thérèse herself. An ambulance had transported him as an emergency case to a clinic in Bordeaux, and from that very day, he began to improve. Thérèse remained alone at Argelouse; but her solitude was such that she began to hear an immense murmuring all around her—as if she were some cornered beast, hunted down and now crouching, waiting for her end to draw nearer—she felt overcome, as if by some frenzied struggle—as if, very close to the goal, her hand already extended to grasp it, she had suddenly fallen to the ground, her legs failing beneath her. One evening toward the end of winter, her father came, beseeching her to exonerate herself. Everything could still be saved. Pedemay had agreed to withdraw his accusation, pretending to be unsure whether he might in fact have written one of the false prescriptions. As for the aconite, chloroform, and digitalis, he would not have prescribed such strong doses; but since no traces of these had been found in the patient's blood . . .

Thérèse recalled the scene with her father, by Aunt Clara's bedside. The room was lit by the fireplace; neither of them wanted a lamp. She explained, in the monotone of a child repeating a lesson (the lesson she had gone over and over during sleepless nights): "I met a man on the road. He was not from Argelouse. He said that since I was sending someone to Darquey's, he hoped I would be willing to include his prescription. He owed money to Darquey and didn't want to go to the pharmacy himself. He promised to come and pick up the medicine at the house, but he didn't leave either his name or address . . ."

"Do better than that, Thérèse; I beg you in the name of the family. Do better than that, poor girl!"

Her father Larroque continued his entreaties stubbornly; the deaf woman, half sunk in her pillows, sensed some mortal threat hovering over Thérèse and began to moan: "What is he saying to you? What does he want? Why are they trying to hurt you?"

She found the strength to smile at her aunt and hold her hand, while like a little girl in catechism class she repeated, "It was a man on the road. It was too dark for me to see him very well. He didn't tell me what farm he lived at." Another night, he came to look for his medicine. But unfortunately, no one in the house saw him.

IX

S aint-Clair, at last. Descending from the train, Thérèse was not recognized. While Balion attended to her ticket, she skirted the station and, passing the stacks of lumber, came to the road where the cart had been left.

This cart was now a refuge for her; on the rutted road, she wouldn't have to fear encountering anyone. But now the whole story she had so painstakingly reconstructed collapsed: out of the whole, carefully planned confession, not one bit of it remained. No—there was nothing to be said in her defense, not even a reason to offer; the simplest thing would be to keep quiet, or only reply to questions. What did she have to fear? This night would pass, like every night, and the sun would rise tomorrow; she would be sure to get through it, whatever happened. And nothing could happen that would be worse than this indifference, this total detachment separating her from everyone else and even from herself. It was death in life; she could taste death, as much as any living being can taste it.

Her eyes growing accustomed to the darkness, she recognized the farm at the road's turning where some low buildings looked like sleeping animals. It was here that Anne, in other days, feared a dog that always ran up and threw itself against her bicycle. Farther on, a stand of alders concealed a dip in the ground; in this spot, on the hottest days, a fleeting coolness would fan the girls' overheated faces. A child on a bicycle, teeth shining beneath a sunshade hat, the bicycle's bell sounding, a voice calling out, "Look! No hands!" This confused image took hold of Thérèse, the only thing she could find from those long-gone days that gave her exhausted heart a little refuge. She repeated a set of phrases mechanically, matching them to the rhythm of the horse's trot: "My useless life—my empty life—solitude with no limits—my barren life." Oh, the only gesture possible—Bernard would not make it. But if he were to open his arms without any questions! If she could rest her head against a human breast, if she could weep against a living body!

She saw the sloping field where Jean Azevedo sat one hot day. To think that she had believed a place existed somewhere in this world where she could have blossomed among people who would have understood her, perhaps admired her, loved her! But her solitude is as much a part of her as is the leper's ulcer. "No one can do anything for me; no one can do anything against me."

✦ ✦ ✦

"Here's Monsieur Bernard and Mademoiselle Clara."

Balion pulled back on the reins. Two shadows came forward. Bernard, though he was still quite weak, had come ahead, impatient to find out for certain. She half rose and called out to him, "Insufficient cause." With no response except "That's that," Bernard helped the aunt climb into the cart, and then took the reins. Balion went back on foot. Aunt Clara sat between the two spouses. Thérèse had to shout into her ear that everything was all right (and in any case, Clara had only a confused understanding of the whole story). As always, the deaf woman began talking at full volume. She said that *they* always used the same tactics, and that it was the Dreyfus affair all over again.[13] "Go ahead, slander away; there will always be something. *They* were rough and strong, and the republicans were wrong to let down their guard. The minute you let up on them in the slightest, the stinking beasts, they turn around and attack you again . . ." These absurdities excused the couple from having to exchange another word with each other.

Aunt Clara, out of breath, struggled part way up the stairs, a candle in her hand.

"Aren't you going to bed? Thérèse must be worn out. You'll find a cup of bouillon and some cold chicken in your room."

But the couple remained standing in the vestibule. The old woman saw Bernard open the door to the living room, giving way to Thérèse, and follow her inside. If she had not been deaf, she would have pressed her ear to the door . . . But no one had to distrust her, already buried alive as she was. So she put out her candle, came back down on her tiptoes, and put her eye to the keyhole. Bernard moved a lamp; his face, so brightly lit, looked both frightened and solemn at the same time. Thérèse was seated, and the aunt could see only her back; she had thrown her coat and hat on the armchair; the fire made her damp shoes smoke. Then she turned her head toward her husband, and the old woman rejoiced to see that Thérèse was smiling.

+ + +

Thérèse was smiling. Walking alongside Bernard in the short interval of time and space between the stable and the house, she suddenly saw, or believed she saw, what it was she now had to do. The very approach of the man had reduced to nothing her hopes of explaining herself or of confiding in him. How completely we can reshape the people we know as soon as they're not close by! During the whole of her journey, she had unknowingly been creating a Bernard capable of understanding, of trying to understand. But as soon as she saw him again, he appeared to her as he really was, a person who had never, not once in his entire life, tried to put himself in another's place, one who had never known the effort to get outside himself and see things the way someone different saw them. Would Bernard, really, even be able to hear her? He paced the low-ceilinged and humid room while the rotten planks creaked under his feet. He did not look at his wife, so full he was with his long premeditated speech. And Thérèse too knew what she was going to say. The simplest solution is always the very one that doesn't occur to us. She was going to say, "I'll disappear, Bernard. Don't worry about me. Right now, if you like, I'll slip out into the night. I'm not afraid of the forest, nor of the shadows. They know me; we know each other. I was created in the image of this arid country where nothing lives, only passing birds and wandering boars. I consent to being rejected; burn all my photographs, and don't let my daughter know even my name. In the eyes of the family, let it be as if I never existed."

And now she opened her mouth and said:

"Let me disappear, Bernard."

At the sound of her voice, Bernard turned toward her. He rushed over from the other side of the room, stammering, the veins in his face swollen:

"What? You want to make a suggestion? Make a promise? Enough. Not a word out of you. You only have to listen, and to obey my orders—to conform yourself to my irrevocable decisions."

As he spoke, he ceased stammering, and his words recombined themselves now into his carefully prepared phrases. Leaning against the chimney, he spoke gravely, retrieving a piece of paper from his pocket and consulting it. Thérèse felt no more fear; she found him laughable, grotesque. Whatever he was going to say in that vulgar accent of his, which would make anybody outside of Saint-Clair laugh, she was going to leave. Why all this drama? How unimportant it would be if this imbecile disappeared entirely from among the living. She noticed his dirty fingernails on the trembling piece of paper; he wasn't wearing cuffs; he was one of those country boys whose absurdity is obvious the minute they pop their heads up out of their holes, whose life has no meaning for any cause, any idea, any person. It's only habit that makes us speak of the infinite value of any man's existence. Robespierre was right, and Napoleon, and Lenin . . . He saw her smiling; exasperated, he spoke more loudly, so she had to hear him:

"I own you: do you understand? You will obey the decisions the family makes, or else . . ."

"Or else what?"

She no longer feigned indifference; she spoke now with bravado, with mockery, crying out:

"Too late! You testified in my favor; now you can't go back on it. You'd be convicted for giving false testimony . . ."

"But a new fact can always be discovered. And I have it in my desk, this new proof. There's no statute of limitation, thank God!"

She shuddered and asked, "What do you want from me?"

He consulted his notes, and during those few seconds Thérèse sat attentive to the prodigious silence of Argelouse. The hour of the roosters was far off; no living water stirred in that desert, no wind blew through the innumerable tall trees.

"I won't give in to any personal considerations. I remove myself altogether; only the family matters. Family interests have always dictated all my decisions. For the honor of the family, I agreed to obstruct the justice of my country. God will judge me."

This pomposity sickened Thérèse. She wanted to beg him to speak more simply.

"For the family's sake, the world must believe we are united and that I never seem to doubt your innocence. On the other hand, I need to protect myself from the worst . . ."

"Do I frighten you, Bernard?"

"Frighten? No. Horrify, yes." He paused, and went on.

"Let's move on and get everything straight once and for all. Tomorrow, we'll leave this house and move in next door, to the Desqueyroux house. I don't want your aunt in my house. Balionte will serve you your meals in your room. You will have no access to any of the other rooms, but I won't forbid you to go for walks in the woods. On Sundays, we'll all go to High Mass in the Saint-Clair church. People must see you on my arm. And on the first Thursday of every month, we'll go to the market in Bazas, in an open carriage, and see your father, just as we've always done."

"And Marie?"

"Marie and her nurse leave tomorrow for Saint-Clair, and then my mother will take her to the Midi. We'll find some health reason for it. You didn't think that we were going to leave her with you? We have to protect her, her too! When I'm gone, she's the one who'll have the property after she's twenty-one. After the husband, the daughter—why not?"

Thérèse leaped up and cried, "So that's what you think—that I did it to get your trees . . ."

Among the thousand secret motives for her acts, this imbecile had been unable to discover even one; instead, he invented one, and the crudest possible one too.

"Naturally, for the trees—what else? One has to proceed by elimination; I defy you to show me any other possible motive . . .

Anyway, it doesn't matter and it doesn't concern me anymore; I'm not asking any more questions. You, you're nothing now; but what still does exist, unfortunately, is the name you carry! In a few months, when everyone is convinced of our happy marriage, and when Anne has married the Deguilhem son—did you know that the Deguilhems have asked for a delay, that they want time to think it over? Well, at that point, I'll finally be able to move to Saint-Clair and you, you'll stay here. You'll be having a problem with your nerves, or something along those lines . . ."

"Insanity, for example?"

"No, that would hurt Marie's chances. But we'll find some plausible reason. And there it is."

Thérèse murmured, "At Argelouse until I die . . ." She moved to the window and opened it. At that moment Bernard knew what real joy is: this woman who had always intimidated and humiliated him—how he dominated her tonight! How she must be feeling the weight of his contempt! And he felt pride in his own moderation. Madame de la Trave had always told him he was a saint; the family had always praised his greatness of soul, and tonight, for the first time, he really felt that greatness. When he was in the clinic and they slowly, cautiously revealed to him Thérèse's attempt on his life, his even temper, which had always gained him such praise, scarcely cost him any effort at all. Nothing is ever truly grave for those incapable of loving, and because he was without love, Bernard had never felt any more than that species of joy that comes from having eluded a great peril, the sort that a man might feel when he learns that he has been unknowingly living for years on intimate terms with a dangerous maniac. But tonight, Bernard felt a sense of his own power; he felt his mastery over life. He wondered at how it was that any problem could resist an upright, right-thinking person; even the day after his torment, he was ready to maintain that nobody is ever unlucky unless it's his own fault. And now this, this worst of events, look how he had *ruled* over it—as if it were just like any other petty problem! People would hardly even know about it; he would save face, and no one would feel sorry for him anymore; he didn't want people's pity. Where is the humiliation in having married a monster, when he was going to be the one who had the last word? A man's life wasn't so bad after all, and the nearness of death had only sharpened acutely his taste for his properties, his hunting, his car, for what he ate and what he drank—in a word, for life!

Thérèse remained standing before the window; she could just make out the white gravel, and she caught the scent of the chrysanthemums, protected from the sheep by wire netting. Beyond, the pine trees were hidden by a black mass of oaks, but their resinous odor filled the night—like an enemy army, invisible but very close, they seemed to Thérèse to surround the house. These wardens, whose piteous complaint she could hear in the wind, would watch her languish through the long winters, gasp during the torrid days; they would be the witnesses of her slow suffocation. She closed the window and turned back to Bernard.

"So you think you'll hold me here by force?"

"In comfort . . . But remember this: the only way you'll ever leave here is in handcuffs."

"What an exaggeration! I know you; don't make yourself out to be worse than you are by nature. You won't expose the family to that shame! I'm not worried."

Then, with the air of a man who has already carefully weighed this possibility, he explained that by leaving, she would be declaring herself guilty. In that case, the only way the family could avoid scandal would be to amputate the gangrenous limb, reject it, deny it in front of everyone.

"And that's the approach my mother wanted us to take right away, imagine! We would have let justice take its course, if it hadn't been for Anne and Marie . . . But now it's late. No need to hurry in giving us your response. I'll leave you now until tomorrow."

Thérèse said quietly, "I still have my father."

"Your father? But we're all entirely in agreement. He has his career, his party, the ideas he stands for. He only wants to avoid a scandal, no matter what it costs. And do think about how much he's already done for you. If the case made against you was sloppy, it's thanks to him. Anyway, he must have expressed his wishes to you . . . No?"

Bernard lowered his voice and became again almost courteous. It was not that he felt the slightest compassion. But this woman, who now scarcely seemed even to breathe, was at his feet at last; she had found her true place. Everything was back in order. Any other man's happiness was nothing compared to this. Bernard was proud of having achieved this reversal. Everybody makes mistakes; everybody did make a mistake, with regard to Thérèse—even his mother, who had, as usual, judged too quickly. It was all because people nowadays didn't care enough about principles; they no longer believed in the perils of an education such as Thérèse had received. True, she was a monster, but still, you also had to add that, if only she had believed in God . . . Fear is the beginning of wisdom. So Bernard saw it. And he told himself how disappointed the townspeople would be, so eager had they been to savor the family's shame, when they saw so united a family every Sunday! He could hardly wait for Sunday, to see people's faces! Anyway, justice would be done. He picked up his lantern, illuminating the back of Thérèse's neck:

"Aren't you going up?"

She seemed not to hear him. He went out, leaving her in the darkness. Aunt Clara was squatting on the first step of the staircase. As she searched his face, he made an effort to smile, and took her by the arm to raise her up. But she resisted, like an old dog in pain lying faithfully at its master's bedside. Bernard put the lantern on the floor and shouted into the old woman's ear that Thérèse was feeling better already, but she wanted to stay up a few more minutes before going to bed.

"You know, it's one of her whims!"

Yes, the aunt knew; it had always been her luck to be going in to Thérèse just when the young woman wanted to be alone. Often, Clara had only had to open the door to feel that she wasn't wanted.

She got up with effort and, leaning on Bernard's arm, reached the room that she occupied above the living room. Bernard went in behind her, took care to light her candle on the table, kissed her on the forehead, and went out. The aunt had not ceased to watch him closely. She could decipher from people's bodies what she could not hear from their lips. She gave Bernard enough time to get to his room, and then softly she reopened the door—but he was still there on the landing, leaning on the banister, rolling a cigarette. She reentered her room hurriedly, her legs trembling, so out of breath that she was unable to undress herself. She remained there, lying on her bed, her eyes wide open.

X

Downstairs, Thérèse remained seated in the dark. A few embers still glowed beneath the ashes. She didn't move. From the depths of her memory, a few scraps of that confession she had prepared during the journey floated up, now that it was too late. But why reproach herself for not having used them? The fact was that that too-well-constructed story had no connection to the reality. All that importance she enjoyed attributing to young Azevedo's words—what stupidity! As if that mattered in the slightest to anyone! No—no, she had obeyed some deep seated, inexorable law: she had not destroyed this family; rather, she was the one who had been destroyed. They were right to consider her a monster, but she in turn saw them as monstrous too. If nothing happened to stop it, they were going to annihilate her, slowly and methodically. "From this day forward, this powerful machine of a family will crush me—for lack of finding some way to slow down the wheels, or to jump out of the way in time. It's pointless to look for any reason except the old, 'because they are who they are, and I am who I am . . .'[14] Masking myself, hiding myself, fooling them—I managed it for fewer than two years, but I imagine others like me could have persevered till their deaths, familiarizing themselves with it, chloroformed by habit, stupefied, asleep at the breast of the maternal, all-powerful family. But me—but me, but me . . ."

She arose, opened the window, felt the chill of dawn. "Why not run away? Just step out over this windowsill . . . Would they pursue me? Would they deliver me to the courts again? That would be the

risk I'd have to run. Anything rather than this unending agony."
Already Thérèse had pulled a chair up the window. But she had no
money; these thousands of pines belonged to her in vain; without
Bernard's intervention, she couldn't touch a sou. As good to hide
herself out in the countryside as Daguerre had, the hunted murderer
for whom Thérèse, as a child, had felt such pity.[15] She remembered
Balionte serving wine to some gendarmes in the Argelouse kitchen.
And it was one of the Desqueyroux dogs that had discovered the
poor man's trail. They had pulled him out of the heather, half dead
with hunger. Thérèse had seen him, tied up on a hay wagon. They
said he had died on the boat before reaching Cayenne. The boat—
the penal colony . . . Were they capable of turning her in, as he said
they would? This proof Bernard claimed to have—a lie probably;
unless he had discovered, in the pocket of her old cape, the packet
of poisons . . .

✦ ✦ ✦

Thérèse decides; she must find out the truth. She goes up the
stairs on tiptoe. As she ascends, she can see more clearly; up here,
the dawn is beginning to show through the windows. Here, on the
attic landing, stands the armoire where the old coats hung—the
ones they didn't give away because they could still be used for
hunting. The faded cape had one deep pocket. Aunt Clara used to
keep her knitting there too, from the days when she would go out
alone to watch for the woodcocks. Thérèse slips her hand inside,
and pulls out the packet sealed with wax:

Chloroform: 30 grams
Aconite grains: 20
Digitalis: 20 grams

She rereads the words and the numbers. To die. She had always
had a terror of death. The key is not to look death directly in the
face, to think only of the essential gestures: pour the water, dilute
the powder, drink it at once, lie on the bed, close your eyes. Try not
to see anything beyond that. Why fear this sleep more than any
other? If she is shivering, it is because the early morning air is so
cold. She goes back downstairs, stopping in front of the room

where Marie is sleeping. The child's nurse snores like a growling animal. Thérèse pushes the door open. The shutters filter the young day. The narrow iron bed is white in the darkness. Two tiny hands are poised on the coverlet. The profile, still unformed, is sunk in the pillow. Thérèse recognizes the oversized ear: her ear. People are right: it's a replica of herself there, deeply asleep. "I'm leaving— but this part of me will stay, with its own destiny to follow out to the very end; not one iota will be omitted." Tendencies, inclinations, laws of the blood, ineluctable laws. Thérèse had read that some desperate people took their children with them into death; good people read about it in the newspapers, and exclaim, "How are such things possible?" Because she is a monster, Thérèse feels profoundly that such a thing is quite possible, and for hardly any reason at all . . . She kneels, and touches her lips lightly to a little hand; she is shocked to feel something surging up from the deepest part of her, rising to her eyes, burning her cheeks: what poor tears, she who never cries!

Thérèse gets up, looks again at the child, moves finally upstairs to her room, fills the glass with water, tears open the wax on the packet, and tries to choose among the three types of poison.

The window is open; the roosters seem to be shredding the fog, a few diaphanous scraps of which hang in the tops of the pines. The countryside is dipped in gold. How can one renounce so much light? What is death? Nobody knows what death is. Thérèse is not certain that it will be a nothingness. Thérèse hates herself for feeling this old terror. She who doesn't hesitate to push someone else over the edge still rears back from it herself. How her cowardice humiliates her! If He exists, the Being (and she saw again the oppressive Corpus Christi procession, the solitary man crushed under the cope of gold, and the thing he carried in his two hands, and his moving lips, and that air of sorrow)—then let Him stop my criminal hand before it's too late. And if it's His will that a poor blind soul crosses through this passageway, may He at least receive this monster, His creature, with love. Thérèse pours the chloroform into the water; its more familiar name carries with it images of sleep and thus less fear. But she must hurry! The house is waking up: Balionte has opened the shutters in Aunt Clara's room. What is she shouting at the deaf woman? Normally, the servant knows she can make herself understood by the movement of her lips. The sound of doors and of hurrying feet. Thérèse only has the time to throw the shawl over the table to hide the poisons. Balionte rushes in without knocking.

"Mam'selle is dead! I found her dead on her bed, with all her clothes on. She's already cold."

Distinctly nonpious though the old aunt had been, a rosary nonetheless had been placed between her fingers, and a crucifix on her chest. Some of the farmers came in soon and knelt and left, but not without gazing at length at Thérèse, standing there at the foot of the bed. ("Who can say for sure that she wasn't the one who did it?") Bernard had gone to Saint-Clair to notify the family and to start the necessary procedures. He must have said to himself that this incident came at a good time and made for a useful diversion. Thérèse looked at the body—the old, faithful body that laid itself down in her path and blocked her at the very moment she was about to hurl herself forward to death. Just chance: coincidence. When people said anything about a specific intention, she shrugged her shoulders. They said to each other, "Did you see? She doesn't even pretend to mourn." Thérèse spoke, though, in her heart to the one who was no longer there: I'll live, then, but like a corpse in the hands of those who hate me. I'll try not to see anything beyond that.

At the funeral, Thérèse played her proper role. The following Sunday, she went to the church with Bernard, who, instead of going down the side aisle as usual, walked ostentatiously through the nave. Thérèse kept her crepe veil down until she had taken her place between her mother-in-law and husband. A pillar kept her invisible to the rest of the congregation; in front of her, there was only the choir. She was completely surrounded by the crowd behind, Bernard on the right, Madame de la Trave on the left, and only that space open before her, like the arena into which the bull enters: a wide space where a man in fancy dress stood between two children, whispering, his arms spread slightly apart.

XI

Bernard and Thérèse came back that night to the Desqueyroux house in Argelouse, which had scarcely been inhabited for years. The chimneys smoked, the windows closed badly, and the wind blew in through small openings that the rats had gnawed. But fall that year was so beautiful that at first Thérèse didn't mind the discomforts. Hunting kept Bernard occupied until night. As soon as he got back, he would sit in the kitchen and eat with the Balions; Thérèse could hear scraping forks and the monotone of their voices. Night fell quickly in October. The few books she had brought from the neighboring house had all been read. Bernard made no response to her request to place an order at the Bordeaux bookstore; the only permission he granted was for her to replenish her cigarette supply. She would stoke the fire, but the resinous smoke blew back at her, irritating her throat, which was already sore from the tobacco. As soon as Balion took away the remains of her rapid meal, she would put out the light and go to bed. So many hours passed as she lay there, without sleep coming to deliver her. The Argelouse silence kept her from sleeping; she preferred the windy nights—that vague sound of lament from the treetops seemed to hide a human tenderness within it. Thérèse let it rock her to sleep. The troubled weather of the equinoctial nights put her to sleep better than the calm did.

Interminable as the nights were to her, she often had to come inside before dusk when a mother, seeing her coming, roughly took her child by the hand and pulled him inside the farmhouse, or when an oxherd, someone she knew by name, did not reply to her greeting. Oh, how good it would be to be able to lose herself, to sink into the crowds of a big city! At Argelouse, there was not a shepherd who didn't know her legend (even Aunt Clara's death was widely imputed to her). She wouldn't dare cross anyone else's threshold; she left her house by a side door, avoiding the other houses; the distant sound of a cart was enough to make her hurry to another path. She walked quickly, with the anxiety of a hunted animal, hiding in the heather to wait for a bicycle to pass.

Sundays, at Mass in Saint-Clair, she felt some respite from that terror. The opinion in the town seemed more favorable toward her. She didn't know that her father and the de la Traves had painted her as an innocent victim who had almost died from the things that had been said about her: "We're afraid the poor little one won't recover. She doesn't want to see anyone, and the doctor says we mustn't insist. Bernard takes good care of her, but she's been hurt in both body and mind . . ."

◆ ◆ ◆

On the last night of October a furious wind from the Atlantic tormented the trees, and Thérèse, half awake, lay listening attentively to the ocean's roar. But at dawn, she was awakened by a different sound. She opened the blinds, but the room remained dark: a thin drizzling rain rustled on the outbuildings' tiles, and on the still-thick leaves on the oaks. Bernard would not go out today. Thérèse smoked, tossed aside her cigarette, and went out to the landing, listening to her husband wander from room to room on the ground floor. The smell of a pipe crept into her room, overpowering that of Thérèse's cigarette smoke, and she recalled the smell of her old life. The first day of the bad weather . . . How could she live through it, in this room with its dying fire? In the corners, the moisture was causing the wallpaper to detach. On the walls, traces still remained of the pictures Bernard had removed to furnish his Saint-Clair room—as did the rusted nails that now had nothing to support. On the mantel was a triple frame of artificial tortoise shell, and the photos in it were as faded as if the dead they represented were dying a second time: Bernard's father, his grandmother, the child Bernard in his "Edward V" haircut.[16] A whole day to be lived through, and then weeks, and then months . . .

When night came, Thérèse could bear it no longer; she opened the door softly, and went down into the kitchen. She saw Bernard sitting on a low chair by the fire; when he saw her, he stood up quickly in surprise. Balion interrupted his cleaning a rifle; his wife let her knitting drop. All three stared at her with such an expression that she asked:

"Do I frighten you?"

"You're not allowed in the kitchen. Don't you know that?"

She said nothing and turned back to the door. Bernard called her back.

"Since you're here—I wanted to tell you that my presence here is no longer necessary. We've managed to create a sympathetic climate in Saint-Clair. People there think, or pretend to think, that you're a bit neurasthenic. It's understood that you'd rather live alone, and that I'll be coming to see you often. From now on, you don't have to go to Mass."

She stammered that it didn't bother her at all to go. He replied that no one was concerned with keeping her amused. Their objective had been achieved.

"And since the Mass, for you, doesn't mean anything . . ."

She opened her mouth, seemed about to speak, but remained silent. He insisted that no word or action of hers could be allowed to compromise their success, as rapid and unhoped for as it had been. She asked how Marie was. He said she was fine, and that she would be leaving for Beaulieu the next day with Anne and Madame de la Trave. He also would be going there for a few weeks, two months at the most. He opened the door and stood aside, waiting for her to exit.

In the dark early dawn, she heard Balion hitching the horses. Then Bernard's voice, the horses pawing the ground, the rumble of the cart passing away down the road. Then the rain on the tiles, on the blurred windows, on the deserted rye field, on a hundred kilometers of prairie and marshland, on the last shifting dunes, on the ocean.

✦ ✦ ✦

Thérèse lit a new cigarette from the end of the old one. Around four o'clock, she put on a raincoat and walked into the rain. She was afraid of the night, though, and she returned to her room. The fire had gone out, and since she was shivering, she got into bed. Around seven Balionte brought her a fried egg and some ham, but she refused to eat it; the taste of fat nauseated her. Always it was pâté or ham. Balionte said she had nothing better to offer her; Monsieur Bernard had forbidden poultry. She complained about Thérèse making her go up and down the stairs for no reason (she had a heart condition and swollen legs). Thérèse was already making things too hard for her; what she prepared was always good enough for Monsieur Bernard.

That night, Thérèse had a fever, and in her strangely lucid mind she constructed an entire life in Paris. She saw again the restaurant in the Bois where she had been, but this time she was with Jean Azevedo and some young women instead of Bernard. She put her tortoiseshell cigarette case on the table and lit an Abdullah. She spoke, opening up her heart, and the orchestra played softly. The circle of attentive faces around her were all enchanted, but not at all shocked. One woman said, "That's just like me . . . I've felt exactly that way too!" A writer said to her privately, "You should write down everything in your inner life. We want to publish the journal of a modern woman in our review." A young man who was in love with her took her back in his car. They drove up the Bois avenue; she was not at all troubled, but instead was delighted with the young lovestruck body on her left. "No, not tonight," she said to him. "I'm dining with a woman friend." "And tomorrow night?" "Not then either." "Your nights are never free?" "Almost never—you could say never."

There was someone in her life who made all the others insignificant, someone whom no one in her circle knew, someone very humble, even obscure; but Thérèse's whole existence turned around this sun, visible only to her, warming only her body. Paris murmured, sounding like the wind in the pines. His body against hers, so light, took her breath away; but she would rather lose her breath entirely than be away from him. (And Thérèse moved as if to embrace him, her right hand clutching her left shoulder—and the nails of her left hand pierced the skin of her right shoulder.)

She rose, barefooted, and opened the window: this dar
isn't cold, but could she even imagine that one day it would
raining? It would rain until the end of the world. If she had mo
she could save herself in Paris; she would go straight to Jean Azevedo and confide in him; he would know how to get her a job. To be
a woman alone in Paris, earning her own living, depending on no
one . . . To be without a family! To let her heart attach itself only to
those she *chose*—not because of their blood but because of their
personalities, and because of their bodies too; to discover her true
relatives, rare and dispersed as they were . . . She slept, finally, the
window remaining open. The cold, wet dawn awoke her; her teeth
chattered, and she couldn't bring herself to get up and close the
window—she was even unable to stretch out her arm and draw up
the blanket.

✦ ✦ ✦

She didn't get out of bed that day, nor did she wash or fix her
hair. She swallowed a few bits of pâté and drank some coffee in
order to be able to smoke (she couldn't smoke on an empty stomach). She tried to recover her imaginary life from the night before;
as the day went on, there were scarcely any sounds to be heard from
the rest of the house, and the afternoon was hardly less dark than
the night. During these, the shortest days of the year, the heavy rain
united and confounded the different times of the day: one dusk
joined another in an unmoving silence. But Thérèse had no desire
for sleep, and her fantasies grew more specific; methodically, she
searched through her past for forgotten faces, smiles that she had
liked from afar, the indistinct bodies of chance encounters, chance
encounters in dreams when her own young, innocent body had been
approached. She was composing a happiness, inventing a joy, creating an impossible love out of bits and pieces.

"She doesn't get out of bed anymore; she doesn't touch her pâté
and bread," said Balionte to her husband soon after this period.
"But I can promise you she empties her bottle. As much as you give
that bitch, that's how much she'll drink. And then she burns the
covers with her cigarettes. She'll end up burning the house down.

She smokes so much, her fingertips and nails are as yellow as if she
dipped them in paint. It's terrible—those blankets that were woven
right here on the property. You just wait to see how often I change
them!"

She said that she was willing to sweep the floor and make the
bed. But that faker up there wouldn't get out of bed. And it wasn't
worth the trouble for her, with her swollen legs, to lug up ewers of
hot water: at night, she'd only find them untouched, right at the
door where she'd left them.

Thérèse's thoughts began to detach from the unknown body that
she had created for her happiness; she grew bored with it, feeling
satiation with her imaginary pleasure—so she invented a new eva-
sion. Someone was kneeling by her bedside. An Argelouse child
(one of those who had fled at her approach) had been brought,
dying, to Thérèse's room. She reached out her nicotine-yellowed
hand to touch the child, and he arose, cured. She invented other,
humbler fantasies: she furnished a house by the seaside, seeing in
her mind's eye the garden and terrace, arranging the various rooms,
choosing each piece of furniture, seeking just the right place for
those pieces she had brought from Saint-Clair, arguing with herself
over the choice of fabrics. Then the décor began to unravel, becoming less precise, until all that remained was a small arbor and a hill-
side facing the sea. Thérèse, sitting up, rested her head on his
shoulder and arose when the clock sounded for dinner, entering into
the shady arbor, and someone was walking alongside her, suddenly
putting his arms around her, drawing her close. A kiss, she thought,
ought to arrest time; she imagined that the seconds were infinite in
love. She imagines it, but she will never know it. She sees the
house, still white, and the well, the creaking pump, the sprinkled
heliotropes perfuming the courtyard; dinner will be a respite before
the evening's happiness and that of the night, so great that it is
impossible to look at it directly, so far beyond our heart's powers it
is. Such is the love from which Thérèse has been more entirely sev-
ered than any living creature has; she is possessed by it, penetrated
by it. She can scarcely hear Balionte's grousing. What is the old
woman bellowing about? That Monsieur Bernard will come back
from the Midi, one day or another, without warning: "And what
will he say when he sees this room? It's a pigsty! Madame must get

up, either on her own or by force." Sitting on her bed, Thérèse gazes in a stupor at her skeletal limbs; her feet look enormous to her. Balionte covers her with a robe and pushes her into the armchair. She feels around for her cigarettes, but her hand falls in the empty air. A cold sun comes through the open window. Balionte fusses about, a broom in her hand, out of breath, complaining about her wrongs—Balionte who, however, is good, because the family always tells how, at Christmas, when the pig she has raised is slaughtered, her eyes fill with tears. She doesn't want Thérèse to reply to her; in her eyes, silence is an insult, the sign of contempt.

But it wasn't up to Thérèse, whether she would speak or not. When she felt the freshness of proper covering on her body, she thought she had said thank you, but in fact no sound issued from her lips. As she left, Balionte hissed at her, "You won't burn these!" Thérèse feared she had taken away her cigarettes, and she advanced her hand across the table: the cigarettes were gone. How could she live without smoking? Her fingers always had to be able to touch those little dry, hot things; she had to be able to smell them, to bathe the room in a fog that had been breathed in and pushed back out through her own mouth. Balionte would not return until evening—a whole afternoon without tobacco! She closed her eyes, and her yellow fingers made the habitual gesture of holding a cigarette.

As seven o'clock, Balionte came in with a candle and put the tray on the table: some milk, some coffee, a bit of bread. "Now, you don't need anything else?" She waited, with malice, for Thérèse to ask for her cigarettes; but Thérèse kept her face turned to the wall.

Balionte had apparently forgotten to close the window properly: a gust of wind blew it open, and the night's coldness filled the room. Thérèse couldn't summon the will to remove the coverlet, to get up, to run with bare feet to the window. Her body huddled, the coverlet raised to her eyes, she remained motionless, only feeling the glacial wind on her eyelids and forehead. The pines' enormous murmur filled Argelouse, but despite this oceanlike sound, it was still the same Argelouse silence. Thérèse thought that if she loved suffering, she wouldn't be so deeply sunk beneath the coverlet. She tried to push it back a little, but could not endure being exposed to the cold for more than a few seconds. Later, she succeeded in lasting a little longer, like a game. Without its being deliberate or voluntary, her sorrow thus became her occupation and—who can say?—her reason for existing in this world.

XII

"A letter from Monsieur."

When Thérèse did not take the envelope held out to her, Balionte insisted: Monsieur must be writing to say when he'll be back; she had to know so she could have everything ready.

"If Madame wants me to read it . . ."

Thérèse said, "Read it! Read it!" And she turned to face the wall, as she always did with Balionte. But what Balionte read brought her out of her torpor:

I've been pleased to learn from Balion's reports that everything is going well at Argelouse . . .

Bernard announced that he was returning, but since he planned to stop in several towns along the way, he couldn't fix the exact date of his arrival.

It will definitely be by December 20. Don't be surprised to see me arriving with Anne and the Deguilhems' son. They were engaged at Beaulieu, but it's not official: Deguilhem insists on getting a look at you first. Observing the conventions, he says, but I think he wants to form an opinion on you know what. You're too intelligent to let yourself fail this test. Remember that you're sick, that your nerves are bad. I'm counting on you. I expect to see you making your best efforts not to hurt Anne's chances, nor to compromise the happy

*outcome of this project that the family finds so satisfactory—just as
I wouldn't hesitate to see that you pay dearly for any attempt to sab-
otage things. But I'm sure I have nothing to fear.*

◆ ◆ ◆

It was a beautiful day, clear and cold. Thérèse got up, obeying
Balionte with docility, and took her arm for a short walk in the garden, though she only managed to eat her chicken breast with effort.
Ten days remained before December 20. If Madame would agree to
help a bit, there was plenty of time to get her back on her feet.

"You can't say that she's unwilling," said Balionte to her husband. "She does what she can. Monsieur Bernard has a reputation
for breaking bad dogs. You know, when he puts the choke collar on
them? It did the trick: it didn't take him so long to turn her into a
cringing dog, did it? But he'd better not count on her staying that
way."

Thérèse in fact was making her strongest efforts to renounce her
fantasies, her constant sleep, her self-annihilation. She was made to
walk, to eat, and above all to become lucid again, to see people and
things as they really were, not as in her fantasy. And when she was
returned finally to this land that she had burned away, when she was
made to tread across its ashes, past the burned and blackened pines,
she would have to talk too, to smile among the members of that
family—her family.

◆ ◆ ◆

On the eighteenth, around three o'clock on a cloudy but rainless
day, Thérèse was sitting before the fire in her room, her head leaned
against the back of the chair, her eyes closed. The shudder of a
motor awakened her. She recognized Bernard's voice downstairs in
the vestibule, and she also heard Madame de la Trave. When
Balionte, puffing and out of breath, pushed open the door without
knocking, Thérèse was already standing up before the mirror. She

applied some rouge to her cheeks and lips. She said, "I mustn't frighten this boy."

But Bernard had made an error in not coming up to his wife right away. The Deguilhem son, having promised his family he would "keep his eyes open," said to himself that "this absence of haste on his part gives you something to think about." He moved a little apart from Anne, turning up the fur collar of his overcoat, remarking that "you never can get these country living rooms heated properly." He asked Bernard, "Do you have a basement below? You know, your floorboards will definitely rot without putting a layer of cement beneath them . . ."

Anne de la Trave wore a light gray cloak, and a plain felt hat with neither ribbon nor rosette ("But even with absolutely no decoration," Madame de la Trave said, "it cost more than the ones we used to wear, with all their plumes and crests. Of course it's the very best felt. It comes from Lailhaca in Bordeaux, but the style is from Reboux in Paris.") Madame de la Trave stretched her feet toward the fire, one after the other, her face appearing both imperious and good natured at the same time, and she turned toward the door. She had promised Bernard that she would be civil but no more than that. For example, she had warned him, "Don't ask me to embrace her. That's too much to ask of a mother. It will be terrible enough for me to have to touch her hand. You see, God knows what she's done is horrible, but that's not what I find so revolting. Everybody knows that there are people capable of murder . . . But it's her hypocrisy! That's what's really horrifying! Do you remember, 'Here, mother, take this chair; you'll be more comfortable . . .' And remember when she was so afraid of worrying you? 'The poor dear is so afraid of dying, that a visit by the doctor would kill him . . .' God knows I didn't suspect anything, but 'the poor dear' coming from her mouth did surprise me . . ."

But now, in the Argelouse living room, Madame de la Trave only felt the embarrassment everyone else was feeling; she observed Deguilhem keeping his eagle eye on Bernard.

"Bernard, you should go and see what's keeping Thérèse. Perhaps she's feeling worse today."

But then Anne—who seemed indifferent, as if utterly detached from whatever might happen—was the first to recognize the famil-

iar steps, and said, "I hear her coming down." Bernard, one hand on
his heart, was suffering a palpitation. He was a fool not to have
come last night, so he could have rehearsed the whole scene with
Thérèse. What would she say? She could so easily ruin everything
without doing anything specific that he could reproach her for. How
slowly she was coming down the stairs! They were all standing,
turned toward the door that Thérèse finally opened.

Many years later, Bernard would still recall the first words that
came into his mind when that ruined body, small, white, heavily
made-up, came through the door: "criminal court." But it was not
because of Thérèse's crime. Instantly he remembered the color picture in the *Petit Parisien* which, among many others, had been
tacked up on the wooden walls of the Argelouse outhouse—and
how, as a child, flies murmuring inside the outhouse and cicadas
creaking outside, he had stared at the green and red picture that represented "The Prisoner of Poitiers."[17]

He remembered that now, as he gazed on the bloodless, emaciated Thérèse, thinking how insane he had been not to get rid of this
terrible woman, no matter what the cost—the way one rushes to
throw water on an overheating machine that, any second, will
explode. Whether she did it deliberately or not, Thérèse always
seemed to carry drama along with her when she came in a room, or
something worse than drama—ambiguity, and the stuff of newspaper gossip: she had to be one of two things, either criminal or victim. On the family's part, there was a murmur of shock and pity so
little feigned that the Deguilhem son hesitated in drawing his conclusions, not knowing what to think. Thérèse said:

"There's nothing to be concerned about. The bad weather has
kept me indoors, and then I lost my appetite. I hardly eat anything
anymore. Better to get thin than to get fat, though. But let's talk
about you, Anne; I'm so happy for you . . ."

Seating herself, with Anne still standing, she took Anne's hands
in her own. Anne contemplated her. Even in that skeletal, wasted
face, Anne could still recognize the insistent gaze that used to irri-
tate her. She remembered saying to her, "When are you going to
stop looking at me like that!"

"I'm so glad you're happy, Anne."

She turned to smile briefly at Anne's "happiness," the Deguilhem boy—at this cocksure fiancé with his receding hairline, his drooping mustache, his stooped shoulders, his morning coat, his short, chubby legs with their striped black and gray trousers (but then, so what! It was a man like all the others; in short, a husband). Then she returned her gaze to Anne, saying to her:

"Take off your hat—ah, yes, now I recognize you, darling."

Very close to her now, Anne saw the slightly grimacing mouth, the eyes that were always dry, always without tears, but she didn't know what Thérèse was thinking. The Deguilhem son said that winter was not so terrible for a woman who loved the interior of her home: "There are always lots of things to do around the house."

"Don't you want to hear the news about Marie?"

"Oh yes—tell me about Marie."

Anne now seemed suspicious and even hostile. For some months now she had often repeated, with something of her mother's intonations, "I would have pardoned her everything because, after all, she's sick. But her indifference to Marie, I just can't stomach that. A mother who takes no interest in her child—you can invent all the excuses you want, but I find it disgusting."

Thérèse could read the young woman's thoughts. "She distrusts me because I didn't ask right away about Marie. How could I explain it to her? She doesn't understand that I'm filled already with myself, that there's no room for anyone else. And Anne herself, she's only waiting to have children and to annihilate herself in them, as her mother did, as all the women in the family do. But with me it's different; I always have to try to find myself again; I struggle to link up with myself . . . Anne will forget her adolescence, and mine, and the caresses of Jean Azevedo, the minute she hears the first wails of her little gnome, more quickly than taking off her coat. The great aspiration of these women of the family is to lose their individual existences altogether. It's beautiful, the way these types give themselves so completely; I can feel the beauty of this self-effacement, this annihilation. But me, but me . . ."

She tried not to listen to what they were saying, trying to think of Marie. The child must be talking by now. "It would amuse me for a few seconds, maybe, hearing her, but it would bore me soon enough; I'd be impatient to be alone with myself again . . ." She asked Anne:

"Is Marie talking now?"

"She repeats everything she hears. It's hilarious. All it takes is for a rooster to crow, or a car horn to sound, and she raises her tiny finger and says, 'Hear the *mujik*?' She's such a love, such a sweetheart."

Thérèse thought, "I have to focus, to hear what they're saying. My head is empty. What's Deguilhem talking about?" She made a great effort, leaning toward him.

"On my Balisac property, the resin workers aren't as sturdy as yours here. They only manage four loads to the seven or eight of the Argelouse peasant."

"With the price of resin today, they must be just lazy!"

"You know, a resin worker today can make a hundred francs a day . . . But I think we're tiring Madame Desqueyroux . . ."

Thérèse had leaned her head against the back of the chair. Everyone rose. Bernard decided he would not be staying in Saint-Clair. Deguilhem agreed to drive, and to send the car back the next day with Bernard's luggage. Thérèse made an effort to get up, but her mother-in-law told her not to.

Closing her eyes, she heard Bernard say to Madame de la Trave: "These Balions, really! I'll let them have it. They think they can get away with this."

"Be careful—don't go too far. We can't have them quitting. For one thing, they've known too much for too long. And then, as for the property, Balion's the only one who knows how to keep it all running."

Bernard said something Thérèse could not hear, and his mother replied, "All the same, be prudent: don't put too much of your trust in her. Watch what she does, and never let her go into the kitchen alone, or the dining room—no, she hasn't fainted. She's sleeping, or pretending to."

Thérèse opens her eyes, and Bernard is in front of her. He's holding a glass and saying, "Drink this; it's Spanish wine. It'll do you good." And as he always does exactly what he has decided to do, he goes into the kitchen, working himself up into a rage. Thérèse listens to Balionte's patois, her shrill protests, and she thinks, "Bernard was afraid, that's obvious, but afraid of what?" He comes back in.

"I think you'll have more appetite if you eat in the dining room rather than in your bedroom. I've given orders for the table to be set with a place for you, the way it used to be."

Thérèse saw anew Bernard as he was during the time they worked together on the legal statement: an ally who wanted, at any cost, to be done with the business. He wants her to recover, no matter what it takes. Yes, it's clear that he's afraid. Thérèse watches him, sitting across from her and working the fire with the poker, but she cannot make out the image his huge eyes saw in the flames: the red and green picture from the *Petit Parisien*, "The Prisoner of Poitiers."

✦ ✦ ✦

As much as it had rained, not a single puddle remained in the Argelouse sand. Even in the heart of the wet winter, an hour of sun was enough to dry the ground out, and to let one go out in espadrilles and tramp along the paths covered with pine needles, elastic and dry. Bernard hunted during the day, returning for mealtimes; worried about Thérèse, he took care of her as he had never done before. There were very few constraints between them. He made her weigh herself every three days, and limited her cigarettes to two after each meal. On Bernard's suggestion, Thérèse walked a great deal: "Exercise is the best way to build up an appetite."

She was no longer fearful of Argelouse. It seemed to her that the pines stepped aside for her, opening their ranks, making a sign for her to feel at home among them. One evening, Bernard said to her, "I'll ask you to wait until Anne's wedding; everyone should see us together one last time; after that you'll be free." That night, she could not sleep, her eyes held open by an unquiet joy. At the dawn, she heard numberless roosters crowing, but they didn't seem to be responding to each other: instead, they sang all together, filling the sky itself with the clamor of their unison. Bernard would let her go free into the world, as he used to let her wander free into the prairies, this wild boar he had been unable to tame. With Anne finally married, people could say what they liked: Bernard would submerge Thérèse in the depths of Paris and take his flight from her. They had reached an understanding: no divorce, and no official separation. They would invent some reason to give people, something to do with her health ("She only really feels well when she's traveling"). He would faithfully send her resin receipts on each All Saints' Day.

Bernard didn't ask about Thérèse's plans; let her go hang herself, for all he cared. "I won't rest easy," he said to his mother, "until she's cleared out." "I'm sure she'll take her maiden name back. And if she gets up to anything, you'll still have to answer for it." But Thérèse, he assured her, only kicked when she was in the traces. Once free, she might become more rational. But in any case, they had to take the risk. This was also Monsieur Larroque's view. All things considered, it was best that Thérèse disappear; she'd be forgotten soon enough, and people would stop talking about her. Keeping silent about it all was the most important thing. Once the idea had taken root among them, nothing could dislodge it: Thérèse must be let out of the traces. And how impatient they all were for it to happen!

Thérèse loved the despoliation that the end of winter imposed on a land already so completely barren; only the tenacious vestment of dead leaves remained, attached to the oaks. She discovered that the silence of Argelouse did not really exist. In the calmest weather, the forest wept the way one weeps for oneself, and then slowly rocked itself to sleep, and the nights were filled with a continual vague whispering. There would be dawns in her future life, that unimaginable life, dawns so empty that perhaps she would come to miss the hour of awakening at Argelouse, with its universal clamor of innumerable roosters. In those summers that were going to come, she would remember the daytime cicadas, the nighttime crickets. Paris—no more tortured pines, but frightening people instead: after the crowds of trees, crowds of men.

The husband and wife were surprised at how little resentment remained between them. Thérèse considered that people become more endurable when we know we'll be leaving them. Bernard interested himself in Thérèse's weight—but also in the things she said, and she spoke more freely to him now than she ever had: "In

Paris . . . When I'm in Paris . . ." She would live at first in a hotel, then perhaps try to find an apartment. She planned to take courses, go to lectures, attend concerts, "to rebuild her education from the ground up." Bernard had no wish to keep an eye on her, and he ate his soup, emptied his glass, without any second thoughts. Doctor Pedemay sometimes ran into them on the Argelouse road, and he said to his wife, "The really surprising thing is that they don't appear to be putting on an act."

XIII

O ne cold morning in March, at about ten o'clock, the human
torrent was already in full spate and beating against the terrace of the Café de la Paix, where Bernard and Thérèse sat. She
dropped her cigarette and, as people from the Landes always do,
she stamped it out carefully.

"You're afraid of setting fire to the sidewalk?"

Bernard forced himself to laugh. He had been reproaching himself for having accompanied Thérèse all the way to Paris. He had
done it for the sake of public opinion, of course, on the day after
Anne's wedding—but even more than that, he had done it in obedi-
ence to Thérèse's wishes. He said to himself that she always had a
genius for creating absurd situations: as long as she remained in his
life, he would continue to be in danger of slipping into irrational
gestures like this one. Even on a balanced personality like his, one
that was so solid, this madwoman retained some traces of her influ-
ence. And now, at the moment of separating from her, he couldn't
overcome a feeling of sadness unlike anything he had ever felt.
Nothing was more foreign to him than a sentiment like that, a feeling that was actually provoked by another person (and certainly not
by Thérèse—it was impossible to imagine it). How impatient he
was to get clear of all this trouble! He wouldn't breathe freely until
he was on the train back to the south. The car would be waiting for
him tonight in Langon. Very soon after you leave the station, on the
Villandraut road, the pines begin. He observed Thérèse's profile,

following her eyes as they occasionally fixed on some figure in the crowd, following it until it had disappeared. Suddenly:

"Thérèse . . . I wanted to ask you . . ."

He turned his eyes away—he had never been able to bear the woman's gaze—and then said very quickly:

"I'd like to know . . . Was it because you hated me? Because you felt disgust for me?"

He heard his own words with surprise and irritation. Thérèse smiled, then looked at him gravely. Finally! Bernard asked her a question, the very one Thérèse would have asked first if she had been in his place. The confession she had taken so long to prepare in the coach all along the Nizan road, then in the train to Saint-Clair, that patient quest, all that effort to work back up to the source of her actions, that exhausting journey deep within herself—perhaps now it was about to be of use after all. She had, without knowing it, troubled Bernard. She had complicated him, and now here he was, questioning her like someone who can't see clearly, someone who hesitates. He was less simple—and therefore less implacable. She gave him a look now that was sympathetic and almost maternal. But her reply was mocking:

"Don't you realize that it was because of your pines? Yes, all I wanted was to get my hands on your trees."

He shrugged his shoulders.

"I don't believe that anymore, if I ever did. Why did you do it? You can tell me now, really."

She stared off into space. Now, on this sidewalk, on the banks of a muddy river of tightly pressed bodies, at the moment when she was about to throw herself in and either struggle or consent to sinking—now she seemed to perceive a light, a kind of dawning, and she imagined a return to that secret, sad country: she imagined a whole life of meditation, of perfecting herself in the Argelouse silence, an interior journey in search of God . . . A Moroccan who was selling carpets and glass bead necklaces thought she was smiling at him, and he made a few tentative steps toward them. She said, with the same mocking tone:

"I was about to tell you, 'I don't know why I did it,' but now I think perhaps I know—imagine that! It was maybe to see some disquiet, some curiosity in your eyes—some trouble, essentially. I've just discovered that, just this second."

He growled, in the tone Thérèse remembered from their wedding trip.

"You'll be a joker right up to the end. Seriously: why?"

She didn't smile now, but asked in turn:

"A man like you, Bernard, always knows the reasons for all his actions, doesn't he?"

"Certainly—of course. At least I think so."

"I honestly wish that nothing had to remain hidden from you. If you knew what tortures I've gone through in order to see it clearly . . . But all the reasons I could have given you, and maybe even the ones I just gave, they all seem like lies to me . . ."

Bernard was impatient.

"But all the same, there was a day, a moment when you made the decision—the decision to do it?"

"Yes, the day of the big fire at Mano."

They had leaned closer together, speaking quietly. At this Parisian intersection, under this thin sun, in this cold wind that smelled of tobacco and agitated the yellow and red awnings, Thérèse found it strange to think back to that suffocating afternoon—smoke everywhere, the azure sky smeared with soot, the penetrating odor of all those burned-up young trees, like so many torches—and in her own sleeping heart, the crime slowly taking shape.

"Here's how it happened: it was in the dining room, which was dark at noon as always. You were talking, your head turned toward Balion, and you forgot to count the drops that were falling into your glass."

Thérèse, in her effort not to omit the slightest circumstance, was not looking at Bernard, but now she heard him laugh, and she turned to him: yes, he was laughing that stupid laugh. He said, "No! What do you take me for!" He didn't believe it—but then, was what she was saying really believable? He chuckled, and she recognized the Bernard who was so sure of himself, who let nobody pull the wool over his eyes. He was in control again; she felt herself lost all over again. He said, as if it were a joke:

"So, the idea just came to you like that, all at once, by the operation of the Holy Spirit?"

How he hated himself for having asked Thérèse questions! He had lost the benefit of all the contempt he had heaped on this madwoman; it let her win, for God's sake! Why had he given in to this sudden desire to understand? As if there were anything to understand with maniacs like this! It had just burst out of him; he hadn't taken the time to reflect . . .

"Listen, Bernard, I'm not telling you this to prove my innocence—far from it!"

She seemed to feel a strange urge to accuse herself. It was clear, she said, that she must have been nursing criminal thoughts in her heart for months in order to act as she did that day, in a kind of sleepwalking. And then, the first act accomplished, what a furious lucidity in carrying out the plan. What tenacity!

"I only felt cruel when I let myself hesitate. I didn't want your suffering to be interrupted; I had to take it to the very end, and quickly. I gave in to a hideous sense of duty—yes, that's what it was like, a duty!"

Bernard interrupted:

"Always these fine, paradoxical phrases! Try, just for once, to tell me what you wanted! I dare you to."

"What I wanted? It would probably be easier to say what I didn't want. I didn't want to keep on playing a role, speaking only set formulas, denying every second a Thérèse who . . . But no, Bernard, look: I'm only trying to be truthful—so why is it that everything I tell you sounds so false?"

"Lower your voice: the man behind us has started to listen."

The only thing Bernard wanted now was to be done with all this. But he knew this maniac: she could have no greater joy than to sit there for hours, splitting hairs. And Thérèse also understood that this man, who had just a moment or two ago approached her honestly, now had receded into an infinite distance. But she persisted anyway, trying on her prettiest smile and putting the low, hoarse inflection Bernard had loved into her voice.

"But now, Bernard, I know that the Thérèse who instinctively crushes out her cigarette with such care, because it only takes the smallest spark to set the trees burning—the Thérèse who used to love going over her resin accounts and figuring out her profits—the Thérèse who was proud to marry a Desqueyroux, to take up her station in one of the good families in the region, happy to tie the knot, as they say—I know that Thérèse is just as real as the other, just as much alive. No, no—it wasn't right to sacrifice her to the other one."

"What other one?"

She didn't know how to reply, and he looked at his watch. She said:

"I will, of course, have to come back from time to time, to see to my business affairs—and for Marie."

"What affairs? I'm the one who'll manage our common hold-ings. We're not going back on what we planned, are we? You'll have your place in all the official ceremonies where it's important for us to be seen together, for the family's honor and in the interests of Marie. In a family as big as ours, there won't be any shortage of weddings, thank God, nor of funerals. To begin with, I'll be sur-prised if Uncle Martin lasts until the autumn; that'll be an occasion for you, and of course you'll have plenty of others . . ."

A policeman on horseback approached, a whistle between his lips; he magically opened some invisible locks, and an array of pedestrians hurried across the black street, after which it was cov-ered again by a new wave of taxis. "I should have left at night, gone out to the prairies, like Daguerre. I should have kept walking, through the scrawny pines of that evil land—walked until I dropped. I wouldn't have had the strength to keep my head under-water in a lagoon long enough (the way that Argelouse shepherd did, last year, because his daughter-in-law refused to feed him). But I could have laid myself down in the sand, closed my eyes . . . But there are crows, and there are ants who won't wait until . . ."

She gazed at the human river, that living mass that was about to open and take her in, rolling her body along with it. Nothing more to be done. Bernard again took out his watch.

"Ten forty-five: time to be heading back to the hotel."

"You won't be too warm for this trip."

"No—tonight in the car, I'll need the blanket."

She saw in her mind's eye the road he would follow, imagined the cold wind bathing his face, the wind smelling of the marshes, of resinous shavings, burning grass, mint, fog. She looked at Bernard with that smile that in other days made women back home say,

"You can't call her pretty, but she's so charming." If Bernard had said to her, "I forgive you; come," she would have got up and followed. But Bernard, having been moved a moment ago, now felt nothing more than a horror for any out-of-the-ordinary gestures, for any words other than those that custom dictates must be exchanged every day. Bernard was "on track," like his carts: he needed his ruts, and when he had recovered them at last, tonight, in the Saint-Clair dining room, he would finally know peace and calm.

"I want to tell you I'm sorry one last time, Bernard."

She said this with too much solemnity, and without hope, one last effort to restart the conversation. But he protested, "Let's not talk about it anymore."

"You're going to feel awfully alone there. Even though I won't be there, I'll still be occupying a place. It would be better for you if I were dead."

He shrugged his shoulders lightly, and told her almost jovially not to do anything about it "for my sake."

"Every Desqueyroux generation has had its 'old boy,' and I guess I'll be it! I have all the necessary qualities (you're the only one who would disagree). My only regret is that we had a daughter, because the name will die out. But then, even if you and I were to live together, we wouldn't want another child. So, finally, everything's for the best . . . Don't get up; stay there."

He hailed a taxi, but before getting in, he hurried back to remind Thérèse that he had already paid for their drinks.

✦✦✦

She gazed for a while at the drop of port remaining in Bernard's glass, then began again to study the faces of the passersby. Some seemed to be waiting, walking off and then turning around and coming back. A woman came past twice, and she smiled at Thérèse (was she a shop employee, or just dressed the way they do?). It was the hour when the fashion shops emptied for lunch. Thérèse didn't consider leaving the café; she felt neither bored nor sad. She decided not to go see Jean Azevedo this afternoon—and she let out a relieved sigh; she didn't feel like seeing him—like having to talk, to search for just the right formulas! She knew Jean Azevedo, but the people she wanted to approach were the people she didn't know; all she knew about them was that they would demand few words from her. Thérèse didn't fear solitude anymore. It was enough to stay here, motionless. As she had imagined her body stretched out in the Midi, attracting ants and dogs, so here she could feel an obscure agitation, a vague turmoil around her flesh. She was hungry; she got up, and saw, reflected in the Old England's shop window, the young woman that she still was. These carefully fitted traveling clothes suited her well. But she retained that somewhat wasted figure from her days at Argelouse—the too-prominent cheekbones, the thin nose. She thought, "I haven't aged much." She ate in the Rue Royale (as she had often done in her dreams). Why go back to the hotel when she didn't feel like it? A warm contentment arose in her, thanks to the half bottle of Pouilly. She asked for cigarettes. A young man at the next table extended his opened lighter toward her, and she smiled. The Villandraut road winding among those sinister pines—to think that barely an hour ago she had wanted to go back and hide herself there, alongside Bernard! What does it matter, to love this part of the country or that one, pines or maples, ocean or prairie? Nothing interested her except the living, nothing except beings of flesh and blood. "It's not this town, built of stone, that I cherish, nor the lectures and the museums, but this living, struggling forest, hollowed out by passions fiercer than any tempest. The moaning of the pines at Argelouse at night only moved me because they sounded so human."

Thérèse had drunk a bit and smoked a great deal. She smiled to herself, exactly as a happy woman does. She touched up her cheeks and her lips with the greatest care; then, having reached the street, she walked off in no particular direction.

Notes

1. The epigraph is from Baudelaire's prose poem "Mademoiselle Bis-touri" from his *Paris Spleen* (1869). The young woman of the title accosts the poet, and it soon becomes clear that she is quite mad, with a bizarre erotic fixation on doctors; in the conclusion, the poet prays for her acceptance in the sight of God who, after all, made her.

2. Locusta of Gaul was a famous poisoner during the reign of the emperor Nero. She administered the poison that killed Claudius, thus clearing Nero's way to the throne. Mauriac compares Thérèse with Locusta, but expresses the wish that he could have made her into a *Saint* Locusta.

3. Peyrecave was the name of the Bordeaux attorney in the case of Madame Canaby. See page 3 in the introduction.

4. Hippolytus is the young huntsman in Jean Racine's *Phaedra* (1677), a modern version of the ancient Greek story, and arguably the greatest masterpiece in all French literature. Hippolytus is the son of Theseus and stepson of Phaedra; in Theseus' absence, Phaedra develops a violent love for her stepson, which leads to the deaths of both of them. Racine makes some important changes to the Greek story: his Hippolytus is in love with the princess Aricia, and when Phaedra learns of this, her incestuous passion turns into a jealous rage. In Euripides' version of the story, there is no Aricia; Hippolytus is a devotee of Artemis, the goddess of chastity and the hunt. Also see page 7 in the introduction.

5. Paul de Kock (1794–1871) was a prolific novelist, whose somewhat earthy, comic novels were widely popular—without, however, enjoying much critical esteem. The *Causeries de lundi* were a popular

series of newspaper articles, chiefly critical and biographical, by Charles-Augustin Sainte-Beuve (1804–1869). *The History of the Consulat* (a period during Napoleon's rule) was by Adolphe Thiers (1797–1877); like the other books mentioned here, it had a wide readership. The point of this list of books is simply to suggest the miscellaneous nature of Thérèse's reading—and perhaps also its conventionality.

6. The wedding of Gamache, or Camacho, is a sequence in the second part of Cervantes' *Don Quixote*, one which formed the basis for a number of later ballets. Gamache is a wealthy country squire, and his wedding is highly opulent, marked by a series of dances and masques; Thérèse's allusion is thus ironic. It is also ironic in that the wealthy Gamache ends up being cheated of his bride—a very pale woman like Thérèse—and she goes off with her true love, a poor man; the contrast with Thérèse's situation is thus emphasized.

7. The guidebooks produced by the German bookseller Karl Baedeker (1801–1859) remained so popular in the early twentieth century that the name Baedeker itself became almost generic for any tourist guidebook.

8. *The Book of Good Stories* was a schoolbook Mauriac himself had read as a child, though it was designed for girls' reading. One of its chief authors was Zénaide Fleuriot (1829–1890), for whose gentle stories Mauriac always retained a somewhat embarrassed affection.

9. Pierre-Jean de Béranger (1780–1857) was an anticlerical and antimonarchical poet whose works were extremely popular in the nineteenth century; the bawdiness of some of his songs contributed to his wide readership.

10. Charles de Foucauld (1858–1916) was a Trappist monk who went to Algeria to live as a hermit, where he was martyred. René Bazin's biography of him was published in 1921.

11. The treatment is named for its inventor, the English physician Thomas Fowler (1736–1801), who developed the mixture containing grains of arsenic for heart patients.

12. This form of the servant couple's name refers exclusively to Madame Balion, who would have been called by her last name (as her husband was), but with the feminine suffix used to differentiate between them.

13. The Dreyfus affair: Alfred Dreyfus, a Jewish captain in the French army, was convicted in 1894 on charges of sending military secrets to the Germans. Dreyfus was widely believed to be innocent, and in fact

the real guilty party was a Major Esterhazy, who was acquitted in a military trial. The affair caused a great deal of controversy centering on patriotism (whether one should support the military and their findings) versus the truth, and Dreyfus' Jewishness became an issue. The controversy divided France deeply, and had long lasting ramifications. In Mauriac's novel, the liberal Aunt Clara would have been among those insisting on Dreyfus' innocence, while the more conservative—and anti-Semitic—Desqueyroux family would have insisted on his guilt.

14. The phrase is adapted from a famous one in Michel de Montaigne's essay "On Friendship," written between 1572 and 1580. Montaigne tries at length to analyze why he had such a feeling of friendship for Etienne de la Boétie and concludes that chance plays the greatest role in such relationships: they liked each other simply "because it was he, because it was I." The essay is one Thérèse would have studied at school.

15. This is one of many instances in which Thérèse's memory is in fact Mauriac's. Mauriac recalled the episode of the hunted murderer Daguerre in his *Nouveaux mémoires intérieurs* (Paris: Flammarion, 1965, p. 59), where he also recalls that it was one of the Mauriac dogs that found Daguerre.

16. The "Edward V" haircut for boys was a late nineteenth-century vogue, following Paul Delaroche's famous depiction (1836) of the young English prince just before his execution.

17. "The Prisoner of Poitiers" refers to a news story that shocked France in 1901: police discovered that the fifty-two-year-old Mélanie Bastian had been imprisoned in her bedroom by her family for some twenty-five years. Photos and drawings of the hideously emaciated woman (who was by now of course entirely insane as well) were in all the papers. André Gide wrote a study of the case, titled *La séquestrée de Poitiers*; a recent reprinting of Gide's study (Paris: Gallimard, 1998) includes reproductions of the kinds of photos Bernard would have seen. Gide's book has also recently been translated by Benjamin Ivry and included in a collection titled *Judge Not* (Champaign: University of Illinois Press, 2003).

"Conscience, the Divine Instinct"

Mauriac's First Draft of *Thérèse Desqueyroux*

This is the first sketch of Thérèse Desqueyroux, whom I originally envisioned as a Christian, making a written confession to a priest.

F. M.

"Conscience,
the Divine Instinct"

W had nothing I could say to you, Father—how could I explain my whole life to you in a few words? And other people were waiting outside—besides my own, there were all these other existences that it was your job to know, to understand, and to absolve, all before you went off for dinner. And each of us ardently desiring that you would be occupied solely with her. A soul who knows her sins, who is lost in a labyrinth of scruples, of remorse, believes herself to be carrying quite enough misery to absorb your entire attention. And it's true that when you lean forward over one of us, you give her the illusion that only she exists for you. Surely this is because you have given yourself no other task but that of resembling, as closely as you can, the heavenly Father ("Be perfect as my heavenly Father is perfect"), and that you have in fact attained this degree of resemblance to Him: giving the gift of your total self to each particular creature. Please don't see any flattery in this: I have only too much need to believe in your omnipotence! Good and evil, the wheat and the chaff are so confused within me that nobody could begin to sort them out, nobody but yourself. I came to you this evening in the hope of finding you free; but people are at your door at all hours, pestering you thoughtlessly. Sometimes you must complain, and say to yourself, "I'm being eaten alive." Sinners throw themselves on you with all the avidity, the ferocity, of an infant seeking the breast. And you defend yourself badly, like a man who knows his house to be the sole depository of bread and wine in a village wracked by starvation. You believe the confessor must not refuse even the smallest child who comes to you with some little scruple regarding the vaguest sin: that's just the way you have welcomed my son Raymond, whom I have reproached strongly for troubling you. But my own importunity surpasses all measure. I came, and I monopolized you for an hour without being able to resolve to make the slightest avowal: you assumed I was in the grip of I don't know what sort of shame, and you suggested I write to you whatever it was I could not bring myself to say: "Write, write, my poor child; don't worry about how many pages it takes; omit nothing . . ." I consented to this joyfully; but first I want you to know why it was that I said nothing. No, I was neither intimidated nor ashamed: only embarrassed; every word I might have used would have betrayed me. How is it that all these people come to know their own sins so clearly? —I don't know my sins. As soon as I opened my mouth, I was about to tell you that I am a criminal and that my crime is of the sort that calls out for human justice, but the words stuck within my mouth: and it was because I was not sure that I had wanted to commit this murder, and not even sure that I had committed it. And anyway, the one of whom I speak is still alive. And yet there is a dead body, a woman's; and do I even know why it is that I carry this weight, this weight that is suffocating me? Are you confused by all this, Father? —I can imagine the tone in which your curé spoke to you about me: "A first-class intelligence, and a noble soul, perhaps a bit melodramatic, but one who always operates on the highest levels." Oh, excellent Monsieur Cazalis! He believes that I have intellectual difficulties regarding the sacraments, and this is why I avoid them. During the Easter season, he redoubled his prayers for me, and he had the more pious parish women include my name in their intentions. I know that he has often applied to me the line from Corneille's *Polyeucte*: "She has too many virtues not to be a Christian."[1] The good man actually thinks I am capable of sitting and worrying about the authenticity of the fourth Gospel.[2] He stammers when I ask him about the silence of Flavius Josephus.[3] If he only suspected how little these things matter to me! I am, in fact, the main reason Monsieur Cazalis asked you to come to our region—so that your learning could supplement his ignorance in these sorts of matters. But Father, don't put any credence into this image of the intellectual woman he has described to you, a portrait that he no doubt thinks flattering to me. Oh, we have so many things to answer for to Someone—I know this so well that no one needs to spend time proving to me that the Judge really exists. I have faith in Him just as much as I do in the fire that burns—the same faith a starving person has in her hunger—that a muddied person has in the water that will wash her clean.

So first, Father, you must know that I had the purest of childhoods. Those ten years I spent at boarding school at Sacré-Coeur—I can see them now shining like a great white field of snow, of light, of joy. But already, maybe, I should take that back: Was I really so happy then? Was I so truthful? I can only view that happiness from the point I'm at now, across the events that have followed upon it, events that no doubt alter it. Everything that I experienced before my marriage now seems in my memory to have been pure. This may only be the effect of contrast with that unerasable dirtying (which is how I view my marriage). The convent, back before I became a wife and mother, seems like paradise to me; a sacred place where no man penetrated; but I was blind to it all then; we don't value most of the things that make us happy until after they've gone. How could I have known that those early years of my life were my true life, that I was closest then to what could have really made me happy? No, I had no idea that my experience of happiness was finished at the very moment when it was just beginning for most of my friends. I told you that I was truthful then. I was: but imagine, if you can, an angel filled with passion—that's what I was, Father. I suffered and I made others suffer, I took pleasure in the evil that I caused to friends and that they caused to me—a pure suffering that no remorse can alter, pure caresses that were in no way criminal. In those days, I believed that you could get pregnant by kissing a man on the lips. Thus my sorrows and my joys were born of the most innocent pleasures. I fear that these childish things will make you stop reading, that you'll throw this letter away. But what followed will demonstrate to you just how far I've fallen from such innocence. Don't worry—I don't belong to that boring species of the misunderstood wife, nor am I getting ready to slander my husband. Anyway, I'm sure Monsieur Cazalis has given you a glowing portrait of him. You can take him at his word: if I remain a complete unknown to the curé, that's not at all true of my husband. He and the curé are alike, two simple hearts made for understanding each other. They're on the same footing. Whenever I repeat to Pierre that he is the only man I love, the only one I will ever love, I am not lying, as God is my witness. But I refrain from telling him that, while I prefer him to all men, just his coming close to me fills me with horror. Then why did I consent to become his wife? Evidently I thought it would be good to live beside him— beside him, not in his arms. Even today, after all these years of misery, I remind myself that he is the best, the most indulgent of friends, at least until the night comes and transforms him into that hideous, huffing and panting animal; but enough. To tell the truth, Pierre is in fact finer than most of the men I might have married. It's not bragging to say that, in our province, the women are superior to the men; we leave our families for the convent at a very early age. At Saint-Sébastien, we find ourselves in contact with young girls who have come from all over France and Europe; we reshape ourselves to fit the best manners of society. Our brothers go off to school too, but they only meet each other there, without mixing with city people and without improving themselves much at all. Their hearts stay with the countryside, and they continue to live there in spirit; nothing exists for them outside of the pleasures it provides for them: the ponds and marshes, hunting woodcocks, boars, and pigeons—and they would be betraying all this if they let themselves lose their resemblance to the tenant farmers, give up the patois, the country inns, the unsophisticated and wild manners. I'm sure that, having seen Pierre and me together, you'd be aware of that contrast that makes strangers say, "What a shame!" But believe me, there's a great deal of delicacy beneath that hard crust of his. And I don't mean only that kindness that makes him beloved by everyone, even by the most defiant of the tenants. "When he's gone, there'll be no gentleman here anymore," they said during that sickness that almost killed Pierre, the sickness I am going to have to tell you about . . . But it isn't just kindness, but a certain integrity that arises out of his good faith: he's one of those men who never speaks of things he knows nothing about, who would never contradict anyone on any subject he wasn't thoroughly familiar with. More than once, I've seen him open one of my books, read a page, and then set it down, saying simply, "I don't understand." None of those exclamations and imbecilic sneers of the kind you hear from people who call anything they can't grasp absurd. He sticks to what he knows and doesn't try to impress people. But sometimes he'll make a remark, on a book or a person, that's so exactly right that I wouldn't dream of disputing it. And at a moment like that, I see in this otherwise extremely modest man a certain movement of pride: nothing flatters him quite so much as a sense of having got something exactly right, and that I've understood that he did, and that I saw it the same way.

"Then aren't you happy?" you'll ask me. But there is another Pierre, unfortunately, the Pierre of the dark—can you understand me? Only a priest, if he's saintly, could see my point. Are you aware, Father, how instinct transforms the being who approaches us into a monster who no longer resembles the man? I read that Descartes had a child by a servant girl. Well, if at that moment, the author of the *Treatise on the Passions* didn't manage to infect that humble girl with his own madness—then at that moment, he was the animal, and she was the angel, the lucid and horrified angel who must have shut her eyes in order not to see him.' I am embarrassed to be drawing your attention to things you have chosen to rise above and avoid even in thought, these criminal delights which to me unfortunately are crimes without delight. But before you judge me, you have to understand my strange state of solitude. The delirium of love only enchants those who are so closely linked and interrelated that they become one, they cannot be separated. But in my case, I've always seen him sinking down into his pleasure while I remain on the bank, mute, frozen. I play dead, as if this madman, this epileptic, could inadvertently strangle me with his slightest motion. And most often, in the midst of his dirty joy he suddenly perceives that he is alone in it: the interminable energy finally is interrupted, and he gets back on his feet, and finds me there as if I were thrown up on the sand, my teeth clenched, cold, a corpse . . . Why did I marry? I won't hide anything from you: you're probably waiting for me to bring up the chaste innocence of little girls, but no: I knew, I knew! Innocent, certainly—but at the threshold of marriage, I trembled, out of instinct, like a sheep in front of the unknown slaughterhouse. My father wanted this match; "like father, like daughter," as they say. Ever since we were born, the whole neighborhood had already matched Pierre and me; it was absolutely necessary that one day his thousands of hectares would be united with the thousands I would inherit. Our peasants, you know, are neither so envious nor so spiteful as not to go into a sort of delirium of adoration when faced with the prospect of two great fortunes uniting into a truly colossal one. But for all that, my father would never have forced me into it if I had shown the least repugnance. I rather doubt that you've ever met and talked with my father since you've come to live among us. That radical anticleric isn't exactly the right sort of game for you; he's so defiant that even Monsieur Cazalis has never dared step through his door. You know that he owns a house in town, another in Langon, and a wine business in Bordeaux. Apart from his business, the only thing that absorbs him is politics; he became head of the local council, and he wanted to get into the Senate, but his rough manners made him too many enemies. Don't worry—I'm not rambling; it's necessary for you to understand how I lived practically as a stranger with this widowed businessman who despises women. For anyone who knows him, there's no better testimony of this contempt than his desire for me to undergo that religious education at Sacré-Coeur; he often says that women deserve nothing better, and it's also true that my mother, during her last illness, had made him promise that I would be brought up in that same convent where she remembered having been so happy. But there is a certain link between this father and me—or at any rate I can only understand myself by seeing this link: this politician, this businessman, a complete stranger to any religious scruple, is nonetheless a moralist in his thinking, and even though he will sometimes hum some refrain from Béranger,[5] I believe he is unusual in being completely indifferent to the attractions of women. My husband's father was a childhood friend of my father. Pierre's father told him that my father, the radical anticleric, was a virgin when he married, and since he was widowed, no one has ever seen him with a mistress. More than that: this sixty-year-old man is pained when anyone touches on indelicate subjects, and even blushes at the slightest allusion to them. He'll leave the table rather than listen to them. But I don't know what impels me to tell you all these things, which will perhaps strike you as pointless.

Please understand me, Father: I can't escape from myself anymore; I'm a prisoner within my own heart. I'm giving you all these keys at random, in the hope that you'll try them all and find that one of them works—that the bolt will shoot back, and that I'll be able to push open the door and be freed.

Why did I marry Pierre? You know what Argelouse is like, where I live today and where I spent vacations as a child—a "quarter," as they call it here, not even a village, really, but a group of farms loosely joined up together out in the countryside. Argelouse is seven kilometers from the town, with only a single communal road leading from it, sagging and full of ruts from the carts, like the roads used to be in France centuries ago, a road that, when you leave Argelouse, shrinks into a sandy path and goes on to die out in this colorless desert—pine forests, marshland, lands where the sheep are the color of ashes. It's a dismal country of shadows, where I've always imagined I could hear the groans of disembodied souls. The best families around here originated in this forsaken region; in the middle of the last century, they established themselves in the village, and their old clay homes became tenant farms. Only Pierre's parents kept theirs in shape for use during the hunting season. And there we found ourselves during the vacations . . . But no—I was on the verge of a lie: during those vacation times, we had a camaraderie of hunting and horses, nothing more. Pierre was timid, too clumsy, too certain of his own defeat to hazard even the slightest approach to me. Monsieur Cazalis used to say, as people do around here, that we were "pretty as a picture" in those days. He loved to watch "the two greatest fortunes in the region" go galloping by together . . . But here I am again on the verge of a lie: The Pierre of those days, a badly dressed Hippolytus, wasn't concerned with girls, only with the hares he could hunt across the fields. Not even a Racinian Hippolytus, because there was no Aricia who could move him to love.[6] He was more of a Greek virgin, bound by vows to Diana the huntress; and I thought nothing more than that about him. I would never have crossed his threshold if his young sister, Raymonde, hadn't been my friend. It will be hard for you, Father, to imagine how childish I was: have you ever heard it said that a girl can love a young man simply because he is the brother of her dearest friend—as I have heard since then, of young men who happily marry the sisters of their best friends? At the convent, Raymonde and I were the only friends who were never separated during the vacations; they brought us even closer together in that region where every road seemed to die off—with no more rules, no more constraints . . . The longest days of the year—how short they seemed to us, under the low branches of the enormous oaks, in front of that country house! Stifled under the crowded pine trees, we went and sat at the edge of a maize field just as we would have done by the side of a lake. We loved to watch the clouds slip by and shift their shapes, and before I had the time to make out the winged woman Raymonde saw in the sky, it had already become, she told me, no more than an elongated animal.

A country of thirst! You had to walk a long time in the sand before getting to the sources of a stream; they were numerous, born out of a hollow among the prairies, between the roots of the alder trees. Our bare feet went numb in the icy water; then we broiled. I still can see a little hut, built as a blind for hunting woodcocks, and the hard, narrow bench where we rested for long, silent, idle moments, and the minutes would flow past without our even dreaming of moving—no more than we would have dreamed of it when a hunter signals us to stand still while the birds approach. And so it seemed to us that the slightest gesture would have startled whatever sort of happiness this was—would have made it flee from us. You probably are assuming that similar tastes brought Raymonde and me together: but no, she couldn't have been more indifferent to the books which made up my nourishment. And I didn't much like galloping along behind hounds, which was her great joy—nor, out in the fields, shooting down larks in full flight. It was like watching a miracle to see her take aim and fire into the setting sun, when the bird's wild cry would break the silence—and Raymonde would pursue the wounded bird across the tufts of grass; she would carry it back, wounded, strangling it with her hands. Later, I would clean off that strong, small hand soiled with blood, with my lips. There was nothing I could say to her. Which of my most secret thoughts would have been at all intelligible to her? And her words were so full of vanity that they buzzed in my ears, and I had no interest in penetrating to their meaning. It was enough for me just to hear her slightly husky voice, a voice they called ugly. Later in my life, I knew boredom listening to intellectual women discoursing to me about the novels I loved, about metaphysics, about poetry. The union of two beings has nothing to do with a harmony of thought, of opinions and beliefs. I feel scorn for people who think the same way I do . . . Nothing matters except that inexpressible concord, that rhythm of another's blood that marries with the rhythm of my blood. There was nothing outside us that brought us together, Raymonde and me, except maybe music. Even today, if I want to evoke the memory of that time, I sit down at the piano at the hour of day when she used to sing the little tunes she loved—I play, and I look at the armchair where she used to nestle with the light behind her . . . All that remains of the world's light seems to me to be caught up in her hair, behind that dear head thrown back, her neck a little too long, a little too muscular . . . But I'm rambling. However, if I've said too much, at least I've said enough for you to be able to picture this childish madness that brought me to marry Pierre. Raymonde and I, we really wanted this marriage to take place, because of all the repeated solicitations and demands that made it clear to us we had to give up all hope of remaining in this happy state we lived in upon leaving the convent. We thought it was wonderful that the marriage, instead of separating us, would unite us. The strange thing is that, once we had resolved on it, I never for a moment dreamed that Pierre wouldn't cooperate, that he wouldn't submit. Since my adolescence, I've had a sense of my power over others— not that I've ever been a flirt. The kind of person they call a "flirt" has always disgusted me. I can't recall ever having made someone jealous, or of having amused myself by hurting someone, or of having feigned either interest or coldness—or any of those ridiculous games. No, no—I walk softly, almost on tiptoe into people's lives; I don't impose myself; and I invade slowly, surely the lives of those over whom I want to have power. Thus, I couldn't even say how I had suddenly become indispensable to the happiness of this boy who, until just recently, had never even looked at me. You understand me well enough to know that there were no physical contacts, and that I was not the sort of girl to seek out the sort of things that would have been horrid to me. But in any case he loved me, felt himself profoundly unworthy of my love, and, no matter how I tried to reassure him, promised to try to conform to all my tastes. Then, whereas his sister would come in and tear a book out of my hands, mess up all my papers, and drag me off into the countryside at siesta time, he would come and question me like a studious child, borrow all the books he'd heard me praise, shave every day, change his clothes for dinner, even give up going to the inn two times a day after he'd heard me say that the very word "aperitif" made my gorge rise. I have no doubt that, if he had known how repulsive I found his hairy wrists and hands, the dear bear would have heroically shaved himself from head to foot. The poor child didn't understand that if I had loved him, I would have loved the odor of his clothes after the hunt, even the smell of his breath after he'd been drinking. The love or repulsion that we inspire in others has almost nothing to do with circumstances we can control. It isn't up to us to be anything but the one the beloved either calls or rejects. Nothing external can make any difference, can add or subtract one little bit from the love or the disgust that we inspire in the other. So, my poor sad Hippolytus tried in vain to make himself into Adonis. His ignorance above all frightened him. I had to agree to a wedding trip of three months. He wanted to visit, submitting to my wise instruction, all the museums in Holland and Italy; it seemed best for me to agree to it. The return to Argelouse in September would only be the sweeter. We left one June evening, in the middle of all the tumult of a half-peasant, half-bourgeois wedding feast. Hundreds of tenant farmers had eaten and drunk to our health; shadowy groups from which young women's bright dresses sparkled cheered us all along our route; we passed carts being driven by drunken boys. The insidious odor of acacias that grew alongside the road is mixed, in my memory, with my first night of what people call love.

You, Father, who have since your youth managed to keep your joy or sorrow from depending on mere appearances, who have felt growing up within you that dark night that St. John of the Cross describes, where everything that is not God is annihilated—imagine if you can the grief of a wife who, having all her life dreamed of certain cities, certain regions in the world, goes to them at last but at the side of a man, a man not exactly detested, but feared more than death itself. And my nights—my nights left me just enough lucidity to be able to imagine what it would be like, how happy I would be, to walk down the steps leading to the station, to lay myself down in one of those gondolas next to a soul I truly loved. And yet the one who really was next to me had scarcely emerged from his adolescence, as I knew only too well. I wasn't entirely indifferent to his youth and vigor, his good looks, his grave and direct gaze, a certain awkward country grace of his that turned the heads of more than a few women and even some men. When he was around me, he was so docile, so fearful, the dear little bear, that I could scarcely believe this was the same cruel animal who had such need of the shadows. It was as if the days were too short for his devotion and concern to make me forget his unimaginable, patient, ill-defined inventions of the nights. A murderer who feels pity for his victim comforts her, and then suddenly, that night, he seizes her . . . Oh, I only did to him what he had done to me, that day when I gave in, bit by bit, to the temptation to kill him, and the desire to save him . . . But it isn't time for this yet—you know some of the causes, but you aren't ready to hear the full horror of the confession. Did he know the evil he was doing to me? He was a child . . . No doubt he had held some indifferent girls in his arms. I considered that he had no point of comparison, and then I thought that perhaps I was the first, the only one. Certainly he had spoken to me of his mistresses, but on that point, men always lie; certain circumstances have led me to think that . . . But here I'm drifting away from my point . . .

Notes

The title comes from Jean-Jacques Rousseau's *Emile* (1762), a half-novel, half-treatise on educating the person into his or her natural goodness. In Book IV, Rousseau exclaims, "Conscience! Conscience! Divine instinct, immortal voice from heaven . . . In thee consists the excellence of man's nature and the morality of his actions; apart from thee, I find nothing in myself to raise me above the beasts." (Translated by Barbara Foxley. London: Everyman, 1995, p. 304).

1. Pierre Corneille, *Polyeucte* (1642–1643), Act IV, scene III, l. 1268. Corneille called *Polyeucte* a "Christian tragedy." Set in the years of the Roman rule over Turkey and Armenia, the nobleman Polyeucte is a convert to Christianity, and in the famous scene alluded to here, he prays for the conversion of his wife, Pauline, daughter of the Roman governor of Armenia; later in the play she does convert, following his martyrdom.

2. Advances in biblical scholarship in the nineteenth and early twentieth centuries had the effect of shaking the faith of many people. One of these advances led to questioning the authenticity of the Gospel of John; the evidence seemed to suggest that it had not actually been written by John, "the beloved disciple," but perhaps by someone in the generation after him. The local curé thinks this is the sort of controversy that is troubling Thérèse, that she is experiencing what were called "intellectual difficulties" with her faith. But as she goes on to explain, the curé is misreading both her and the nature of her unhappiness.

3. Flavius Josephus, who lived from AD 37 to around 93, wrote two major works on Jewish history, but he only mentions the story of

Jesus' death briefly, and gives no attention at all to the small sect of Christians in his day. Thus, a modern anti-Christian can cite Josephus as objective, contemporary testimony regarding how unimportant Jesus of Nazareth really was in the era, testimony that suggests Christian belief is the product of later generations.

4. René Descartes' *Les Passions de l'âme* (1650) is a discussion of how body and mind interact and affect each other. Descartes was one of the greatest exponents of mind-body dualism, so it is appropriate that Thérèse thinks of him here.

5. Pierre-Jean de Béranger: see note 9 on page 126.

6. Hippolytus: see note 4 on page 125.

About the Author

François Mauriac, born in Bordeaux in 1885, became one of the greatest novelists of his generation. A series of highly successful novels in the 1920s led to his election to the French Academy in 1933. Mauriac's novels, those from both the 1920s and later, are swiftly paced psychological studies of individuals in crisis; he places these characters within a Catholic framework, so that questions of sin, grace, and redemption are always central. He also wrote reviews, criticism, poetry, plays, and biographies. During World War II he wrote for the French Resistance under the pseudonym Forez, and after the war he continued to work prolifically as both a novelist and a journalist. He was awarded the Nobel Prize for Literature in 1952. He divided his time between Paris and the family home in the countryside near Bordeaux, where most of his novels are set. He died in Paris in 1970.

Raymond N. MacKenzie, professor of English at the University of St. Thomas in St. Paul, Minnesota, has translated Mauriac's *God and Mammon* and *What Was Lost*. He is also author of a biography of the novelist Viola Meynell and has published a number of articles on literature, ethics, and publishing history.

Joseph Cunneen, cofounder and longtime editor of the ecumenical quarterly *Cross Currents*, is the author of *Robert Bresson: A Spiritual Style in Film* and translator of plays by Gabriel Marcel and two books by the French priest-novelist Jean Sulivan.

Made in the USA
Monee, IL
06 January 2024

51299893R00089